The Spectacular Gift

and Other Tales from Tell Me a Story

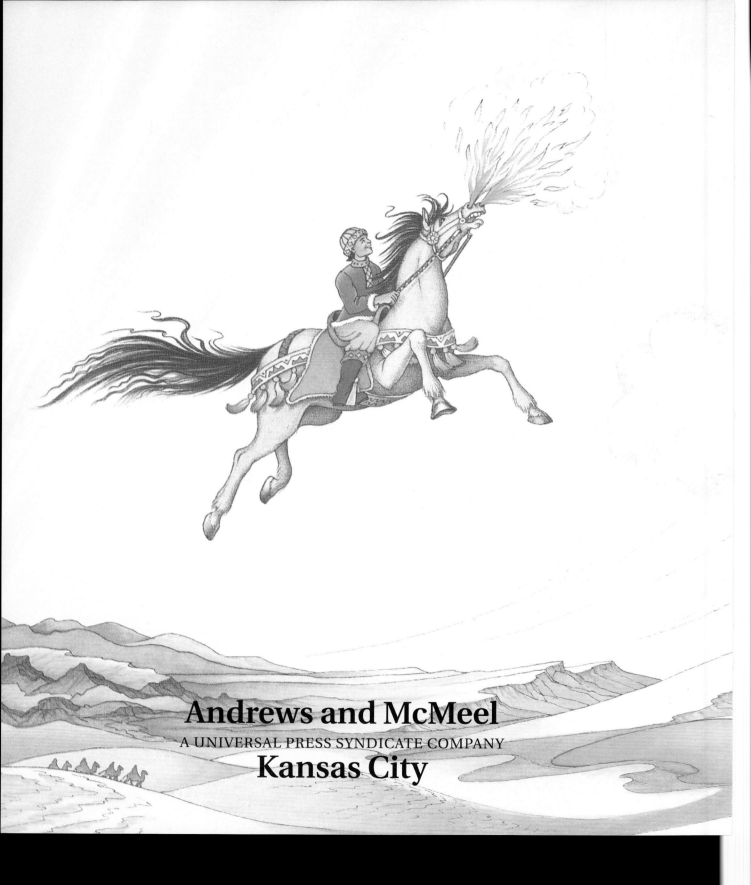

Andrews and McMeel

A UNIVERSAL PRESS SYNDICATE COMPANY

Kansas City

The Spectacular Gift

and Other Tales from Tell Me a Story

Adaptations by Amy Friedman
Illustrated by Jillian Hulme Gilliland

For HARRIET CHOICE and ALAN McDERMOTT

Library of Congress Cataloging-in-Publication Data

Friedman, Amy.
    [Best bedtime stories. Selections]
    The spectacular gift and other tales from Tell me a story / adaptations by Amy Friedman : illustrated by Jillian Hulme Gilliland.
        p.   cm.
    Summary: Presents more than twenty traditional tales from around the world, including "Little Mouse Marries," "The Clever Girl," "Kerplunk," and "The Star Maiden."
    ISBN: 0-8362-0746-7 (hard cover)
    1. Tales. [1. Folklore.] I. Gilliland, Jillian Hulme, 1943- .
II. Title.
    PZ8.1.F897Sp 1995
[398-2]--dc20   95-41105
                                                   CIP
                                                   AC

Contents

Introduction

One night at dinner, a skeptical friend of ours said to us, "There's no such thing as a talking moon or a moon that can read."

After dinner we took him outside and stood beneath a halo of stars. "Listen," we said. "Be very quiet." We stood silently, listening to the voices around us. We listened to the owls and night birds. We heard the patter of feet upon the cooling earth, the chatter of chipmunks settling down to sleep. Soon the moon began to rise.

Our friend smiled at us. "Maybe I was wrong," he said. "Shhh, I think I hear something."

We three sat on the grass listening for what seemed like hours. "You know," our friend said, "when I listen hard, I begin to hear things I've never heard before."

Inspired by the stories he heard in the night sounds, our friend began telling tales of his own. The next night we shared with him other tales we had heard. Before too many nights had passed, another friend joined us, and then another and another—until at last we were sharing stories that seemed to be never-ending. And each morning the world was a little brighter.

"It doesn't matter who tells the story," our friend said. "It's the stories that matter."

We nodded in agreement. "Yes, we know."

Because we *do* know that stories open our eyes and ears and all of our senses to a deeper understanding of people, animals, the sun, the moon, the stars. Tales speak to our visions, our dreams, our imaginations. Stories make us laugh and cry and look and listen hard. And because we possess such a rich heritage of stories, we are richer in human and cultural values. Some of these stories, in fact, come from nations and even languages that no longer exist except in their tales.

Stories make these cultures come alive again.

We hope these stories will make you rich beyond measure—rich in hopes and rich in dreams and rich in understanding of the world in which you live.

They are indeed a spectacular gift.

Amy Friedman and Jillian Gilliland
Kingston, Ontario, Summer 1995

Tell Me a Story

ONCE LONG AGO, as darkness descended,
Stars lit the sky and Bear knew day had ended.
So he smiled to himself, for the kids would come soon,
And the folks would read stories 'neath the light of the moon.

Bear loved books about witches and books about fairies.
He loved books about fine fellows hoping to marry.
Bear loved books about unicorns, books about ants.
He loved books about other bears, dragons, and plants.

Alas, Bear didn't know that the folks were away,
Traveling around for a week and a day.
They left Bear at home, for Bear was a toy,
Though books for Bear too were a treasure, a joy.

He lay down and fluffed up the pillow 'neath his head,
And while he was waiting, 'twas this that he said:

> Tell me a story under the stars.
> Tell me a story from here and afar.
> Tell me a story of every land,
> Tell me a story—oh, stories are grand!

Time passed and he heard not a word, not a sound.
Bear climbed to the window, Bear looked to the ground.
"Where are you, kids? Parents, where are you?" he shouted.
Then he looked to the sky, and there too he scouted.

Tell me a story from Australia and China.
Tell me a story—nothing could be finer!
Tell me a story from Peru, from Japan,
Tell me a story from Persia—that's Iran!

And Moon heard Bear's call, so he woke and he rose
Up to the window where Bear stood on his toes.

Bear smiled, "Oh hello, Moon. I'm surprised at your light.
How pleasant to see you on this very sad night.
Seems my family is away and there's no one to read
All the books in our room, all the stories I need."

"But Bear, don't be sad," said Moon cheerfully.
"Tonight is a grand night—a night filled with me!
We'll fly to the stars and we'll see the whole world.
And I'll tell you a story to make your fur curl."

"Oh no!" exclaimed Bear. "Moon, you must read a book.
Over here, on the bed. Just peek in, take a look.
Tell me a story, oh, won't you please, Moon?
Oh, Moon, if you will, I will go to bed soon."

Now Moon hemmed and hawed and said, "Bear, I don't know,
If I can read all of these words in a row."
Bear looked up at Moon with a questioning gaze
And wondered if Moon might just be in a phase.

"It's easy," said Bear, "I know you can do it.
Try Father's eyeglasses.
Here, see, just look through it."

So Moon, feeling queasy, took the glasses to wear,
And he opened a book, and he looked. Did he dare?
Try to read all these tales? These stories so dear?
He turned the first page, and Bear waited to hear.

And lo and behold, Moon could read a whole story!
And lo and behold, Moon was now in his glory.

Moon read about knights, about ladies and gents.
Moon read about nomads, their travels, their tents.

Bear picked up the book about grand Camelot,
About Arthur and Gawain and brave Launcelot.

Moon smiled as he read about Guinevere and Merlin,
And they traveled toward England, Moon rocking and swirlin',
Telling the stories of magic and potions.
And Bear listened closely as they sailed over oceans.

Bear loved dear Moon for his fine reading style,
And suddenly Bear looked at Moon with a smile.
"Time now for milk, Moon, and time for a cookie,
You're a fine reading Moon, though you say you're a rookie."

And now Moon was ready to take a long flight
He sailed quickly east, straight into the night.
And he opened a book, and said, "We will read, Bear!"
And here are the stories they wanted to share.

The Fairy and the Spider

LONG, LONG AGO, in a land not far away from here, the silver moon shone brightly over the vast, cold land. The stars twinkled above, and the people slept, wrapped beneath thick, warm blankets. And while the world lay so peacefully, a fairy carrying a heavy bundle of dreams was hurrying home. She had spent many hours collecting her great bundle of lovely dreams. Now at last she had enough for all the people.

Looking up at the moon to check the time, she suddenly realized that she would have to hurry if she were to return home on time. The Fairy Queen had been quite clear: "Be home before dawn, my fairies, else we will have no dreams to disperse to your people."

Now the fairy began to run. In her haste she tripped over tree roots and scraped her shins against the sharp wild rosebushes. "Hurry, hurry," she said to herself, and then, suddenly, she ran smack into a spiderweb.

The web held her fast. Sticky silver threads clung to her wings. She turned to twist free and another thread caught her. She struggled and struggled, turning this way and that. At last she saw it was no use. She was caught. She burst into frustrated, angry tears and her bundle of dreams fell to the ground.

She could do nothing but lie still and wait for dawn. It came suddenly, dazzling displays of red and gold, and woke the tired fairy.

The daylight woke Mrs. Spider

as well. Crawling out of her den, she caught sight of the fairy. "What's this?" she cried. "A new kind of fly! How lovely!"

The fairy was quite insulted. "Mrs. Spider," she said angrily, "I am not a fly at all. I am a little fairy and I flew into your web last night in my haste to return home."

Mrs. Spider frowned. "Just a fairy!" she said crossly, "I suppose you are one of those fairies who help the flies to fly away from me."

"I help anyone in trouble," the fairy said gently.

"And now that you are in trouble," snapped Mrs. Spider, "I am sure the flies won't come to help you."

Now the fairy was quite certain this was true, but she hoped Mrs. Spider would be kind. "Won't you help me?" she asked, as sweetly as she could. She began to weep. "The Fairy Queen likes me. The Fairy Queen trusts me. Who will do my work if I am gone? Tell me that."

Mrs. Spider stood very still and watched the fairy's teardrops fall like dew on the silver threads of her web. The sunbeams lit the drops so that they glistened like the Fairy Queen's diamonds. Mrs. Spider was dazzled and amazed. "Your tears are beautiful," she said under her breath. "And just what sort of work is it that you do?" she asked.

At that the fairy stopped crying, for she remembered all the wonderful errands she had long performed. "Once," she said, "I set free a beautiful mockingbird trapped in a cage."

"Why free a mockingbird?" asked Mrs. Spider.

"Oh, if you had only heard him sing," sighed the fairy. "His voice was like a thousand angels' voices, but in the cage he stopped singing. He longed for his home, for the lovely treetops and the freedom of the bright, blue skies."

The fairy smiled to herself, remembering the mockingbird's song. "Listen," she said. "I will sing you a song that might lighten your heart."

And she burst into song.

> Oh! listen well, and I will tell,
> Of the land where the fairies dwell;
> The lily bells ring clear and sweet
> And green grass grows beneath your feet
> In the land where fairies dwell.
> In the land where fairies dwell.

Now Mrs. Spider felt calm and peaceful, for she adored music. She begged the fairy to go on.

> There's love, sweet love, for one and all
> For love is best for great and small
> In the land where fairies dwell,
> In the land where fairies dwell.

Mrs. Spider was so moved by the music that she could not help herself. "Here," she said, "I will help set you free," and she showed the fairy how to break the slender threads, one by one.

When the little fairy was free at last, she reached down and picked up her bundle of dreams. "Now, dear friend," she said, looking with gratitude at Mrs. Spider, "what can I do for you?"

Mrs. Spider thought and thought. At last she smiled to herself and said, "I only wish you to sing me a song now and then."

"Very well," said the little fairy, and off she flew home.

Now as it happened, when she arrived, the Fairy Queen approached her. "My trusted fairy," she said, "I've been so worried about you that I can't be angry. Besides, I need a glorious dress for the grand ball."

The fairy smiled. "I know where I can find some lace and a wonderful spinner," she told the Queen.

"Go then," said the Queen. "Bring the spinner to me, and tell her she too may attend the ball and sit at my table."

The little fairy flew back at once to see Mrs. Spider. "You are invited to Fairyland to spin for the Queen," she said. "And you will be her guest at the grand ball."

"Will there be music?" asked Mrs. Spider.

"The greatest music you will ever hear," said the fairy.

When Mrs. Spider finished the dress, it was the most beautiful that anyone had ever seen. Of course, the Fairy Queen rewarded her with a position as the court spinner, and from that day on Mrs. Spider heard the fairies singing every single day as they carried their dreams to the people. Hearing their music, she was filled with love and happiness.

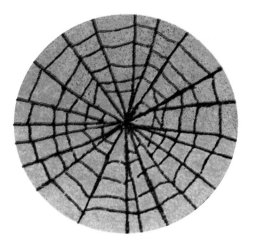

The Pot of Honey
and the Big, Fat Cheese

ONCE UPON A TIME, in a faraway land, Uncle Bear kept to himself a pot of honey and a big, fat cheese. Mr. Fox kept no cheese and no honey. Mr. Fox kept nothing at all but his wits.

Now, Mr. Fox decided that it might be very fine indeed if he and Uncle Bear went into partnership. "Uncle Bear," said he, "a head full of wits like mine is worth far more than your pot of honey and your big, fat cheese."

Now that was true, except that folks cannot share wits the way they can a pot of honey and a big, fat cheese. Folks cannot share wits the way they might share a bushel of corn or a plate of salami and eggs. No, wits are hard to share, but all the same Uncle Bear agreed to go into a partnership with Mr. Fox.

So that's what they did. "Now how do we divide things?" asked Uncle Bear.

"We'll use the wits for now," said Mr. Fox, "and save the pot of honey and the big, fat cheese for later when we need them."

"For a rainy day," said Uncle Bear.

They shook on that.

A few days after Mr. Fox and Uncle Bear went into partnership, Mr. Fox felt hungry for honey. He and Uncle Bear were sitting in their cozy den, and Mr. Fox said, "Uncle

Bear, I'm feeling under the weather today. I think I'll just go off to see the Brother Doctor."

"Very well," Uncle Bear said, and off went Mr. Fox. But he didn't go to the doctor. No, he went to the storehouse, sat right down, and stuck his snout into the honey jar. And he gobbled up a fair bit of Uncle Bear's share of the partnership. Then he lay down in the warm sunshine and bathed and sighed deeply. "Oh," said he, "a sunbath is very pleasant, especially after such a mouthwatering meal."

Mr. Fox awoke and returned to the den, and Uncle Bear said, "How do you feel now, partner?"

"Oh, well enough," said Mr. Fox.

"And did you take some bitter medicine?" asked Uncle Bear.

"Oh no, it was good," sighed Mr. Fox.

"And how much did the doctor give you?" asked Uncle Bear.

"Oh, one part of a potful," said Mr. Fox.

Uncle Bear thought to himself, Oh my, that's a great deal of medicine to take.

Things went smoothly until another day came along and Mr. Fox was hungry for honey once again, so he said, "I have to go over yonder and visit my aunt," and waving good-bye to Uncle Bear, he trotted directly to the storehouse, and there he ate up a great deal of the honey, and he slept for awhile in the sun. Then he went back to the den.

Uncle Bear asked, "And did you see your aunt?"

"Oh yes," said Mr. Fox.

"And did she give you anything?" asked Uncle Bear.

"Oh yes," said Mr. Fox.

"And what was it she gave you?" asked Uncle Bear.

"Why, she gave me something of a pot," said Mr. Fox.

And Uncle Bear thought to himself, Oh dear! That is a strange gift for an aunt to give her nephew.

A few days more passed and pretty soon Mr. Fox was thinking of honey again. This time it was a christening he had to attend, and he went to the pot of honey, and this time he finished it off. He took a nap in the sun and returned to the den.

Uncle Bear asked, "Did everything go smoothly at the christening?"

"Oh, smoothly enough," said Mr. Fox.

"And did they have a christening feast?" asked Uncle Bear.

"Oh, yes," said Mr. Fox.

"And what did they serve?" asked Uncle Bear.

"Oh, everything in the pot," said Mr. Fox.

Dear, dear, thought Uncle Bear, they must have been a hungry bunch to eat a whole big pot.

So a while passed, and one day Uncle Bear got a craving for some honey, so he said to Mr. Fox, "Let's have a feast. We'll invite Father Goat to our place and eat up the pot of honey and the big, fat cheese."

The idea pleased Mr. Fox, so Uncle Bear went to invite Father Goat to come to eat the honey and the cheese, and off trotted Mr. Fox to the storehouse.

"See, now," said Mr. Fox to himself as he stood in the storehouse, "the pot of honey and the big, fat cheese belong together. It would be a pity to part them." So he sat down and in less time than it took to say, "We'll make a partnership," the cheese was all inside him.

Mr. Fox returned to the den, and there sat Father Goat toasting his toes at the fire, awaiting supper. And there stood Uncle Bear on the back doorstep sharpening the big bread knife.

"Hello!" said Mr. Fox to Father Goat. "What are you doing here?"

"Waiting for supper, that is all," said Father Goat.

"And where is Uncle Bear?" asked Mr. Fox.

"He's sharpening the bread knife," said Father Goat.

"Yes," said Mr. Fox, and then he whispered, "when he is through with that, he says he is going to cut off your tail."

Dear, dear! but Father Goat was frightened. He thought, "This is no place for me!" So off he marched, right out the front door. Mr. Fox went out to Uncle Bear and said, "That was a fine friend you asked to sup with us."

Uncle Bear looked up from his knife and said, "Why? What do you mean?"

"Oh ho," said Mr. Fox, "that sneaky Father Goat has marched off with our pot of honey and our big, fat cheese, and we will sit down and whistle over an empty table."

When Uncle Bear heard this, he at once got up, and off he went after the thief. "Stop! stop!" he bawled, "Let me have a little, please . . . Father Goat, let me have just a little . . ."

And Father Goat thought that Uncle Bear was speaking of his tail, for he knew nothing of the honey or the cheese. So he knuckled down and ran until the gravel flew up behind him.

So nothing was left of the partnership but Mr. Fox's wits, for nobody could say that Father Goat carried off any wits.

The pot of honey and the big, fat cheese were gone, and no one can live on thin air. That's the truth. So Uncle Bear and Mr. Fox sat down to think. But that's another story altogether.

Apple Picking

UNCLE BEAR and Mr. Fox had a partnership, but between them all they owned was Mr. Fox's wits. So one day Mr. Fox had an idea. "See now," says he, "Farmer John over yonder has a storehouse full of sausages and puddings and all sorts of good things. As we have nothing to make our partnership equal, we'll have to churn our wits a bit and see if we can make some butter."

"That suits me fine," says Uncle Bear. So off they march, arm in arm, to Farmer John's.

By and by they come to the old farmer's house, and no one is around. And there before their eyes, as plain as the nose on your face, is the storehouse full of sausages and puddings and other good things. Only the door is locked. However, there is a window big enough for Mr. Fox to slip through, though it is up high. "Just lift me up through the window," says he to Uncle Bear, "and I will drop the good things out for you to catch."

So Uncle Bear gives Mr. Fox a leg up and he's in the storehouse, happy as a pig in mud, or a mouse in a cheese box, or a child in a free candy store. "What shall it be first, sausages or puddings?" Mr. Fox calls out loudly. "Hush! Hush!" says Uncle Bear.

"Yes, yes," shouts Mr. Fox, louder than ever. "Only tell me which I shall take first. Shall it be sausages or puddings?"

"Shh!" hisses Uncle Bear. "If you make noise, you will alert Farmer

John, and he and his men will come running. Just take the first thing you see and be quick!"

"Yes, yes," bawls Mr. Fox as loud as he is able. "But I see everything. Tell me which I shall take first."

Well, you can imagine, Mr. Fox is making such a hubbub that in the next moment Farmer John and all his men come running, and with them are two big dogs.

"Ha!" they say, "There's Uncle Bear after our sausages and puddings!" And there is nothing for Uncle Bear to do but step on it and run. He runs and runs, fast as he can, but all the same, they catch him on top of the hill and hurt him so much that for days his bones ache.

Meanwhile, Mr. Fox just waits until all the others are well away on their own business and he fills bags with the best of the stuff. He opens the door from the inside and walks out as though he owns the place.

Then Mr. Fox hides the good things away in a place of his own and returns to the den. And he's groaning as though he's had an awful beating. Oh, he moans and groans so long and loud that even the stones are weeping. "Dear, oh dear, what a beating I've had!" says he.

"And so have I," says Uncle Bear, holding his paw to his head.

"See now," says Mr. Fox, "this is what comes of going into partnership and sharing my wits with you. If you had only made your choice when I asked you, our butter would not have been spoiled in the churning."

Poor Uncle Bear. Still, he is not the first one in the world who has lost his supper and had a beating and gotten the blame in the bargain.

17

Nothing lasts forever, and by and by Mr. Fox finishes all the good things from Farmer John's storehouse and he's without anything in his larder. "Listen," he says to Uncle Bear, "I saw them storing the apples at Farmer John's, and if you have a mind to try the wits that belong to us, we'll go and fetch a bagful apiece."

That suits Uncle Bear, so off they march, each with an empty bag to fetch apples. They come to Farmer John's and no one is about, but this time the door is unlocked, so both of them go in and begin to fill their bags.

Mr. Fox tumbles apples into his bag as fast as he can, just as they come, good or bad. But Uncle Bear takes his time and picks them all over, for he is bound and determined to get the best. So soon Mr. Fox has a bagful of apples, but Uncle Bear has picked only a few and he's rolling each juicy apple around, feeling and sniffing and looking.

"I'll just peek out the window," says Mr. Fox, "to see if Farmer John is coming." But to himself he says, "I'll slip outside and turn the key of the door and lock Uncle Bear inside and somebody will blame him for this. He is stronger and tougher than I, and he will never fit through this window."

So up he jumps to the window, holding his bag full of apples. But Farmer John has set a trap up there to catch rats. Up jumps Mr. Fox, and click! The trap catches him by the tail, and there he hangs from the window.

By and by, Uncle Bear looks up. He laughs. He yells out, "Is Farmer John coming?"

"Hush! hush!" says Mr. Fox. He is twisting and turning, trying to get out of the trap. Now the shoe is on the other foot.

"Yes, yes!" cries Uncle Bear, louder than before, "but tell me, is Farmer John coming?"

"Shhh!" says Mr. Fox. He twists and turns, but it's no use.

"Did you hear me?" bawls Uncle Bear, loud as he can. "Is Farmer John coming?"

Yes, he is. For Farmer John has heard the hubbub once again, and here he comes with his men and his big dogs.

"Oh, Farmer John," sobs Mr. Fox, "I am not the thief. Uncle Bear is in the storehouse. He's the culprit!"

Farmer John knows. Here's the rogue of a fox caught in his trap and he says, "You are the thief! We'll beat you black and blue!" And Mr. Fox hears this and pulls with all his might, and part of his tail snaps off. And away he flies, with Farmer John and the men and the dogs after him.

Now Uncle Bear fills his bag full of apples, and pretty soon he walks quietly out the door and goes home.

And that is how Mr. Fox came to have such a short tail.

What is the meaning of all this? What do you think?

The Spectacular Gift

ONCE UPON A TIME a king had three handsome and clever sons. They loved their father, and they loved each other, but, alas, when they grew to be of marrying age, all three brothers fell in love with the same young woman, a princess from a neighboring village. The princes decided to visit the princess's father and ask him to choose the son he liked best. Whoever the king chose would marry the princess.

The first son bowed low to the king and said, "Sir, I wish to marry your delicate daughter, the princess."

The second son bowed lower and said, "Good king, I too wish to marry your daughter. I promise I will be a fine husband."

And the third prince bowed still lower and he said, softly, "Dear king, I love the shy princess with all my heart, and if you give me your permission to marry her, you will make me the happiest man in all the world."

The king looked at all three lads and saw that each was good and true. He did not wish to favor one over the other, and so he devised a contest. "Whichever of you brings to me the most spectacular gift will marry my daughter," he said.

And so the princes set off into the world to search for a spectacular gift for the king. They traveled together for a while and then, on the far side of the highest mountain, they parted ways.

The eldest prince walked at once into the city, for he believed the city held the most spectacular things in the world. He walked along the cobbled streets, looking closely into every shop and stall. He examined exquisite jewels, marvelous music boxes, sets of fine china. Each gift was beautiful, but none was more spectacular than all the rest.

When he came upon a merchant selling rugs, he smiled at the rug seller and said, "I seek the most spectacular gift in the world."

"Ahh," said the merchant, "then you'll want to purchase this carpet." He pointed to a thin, worn rug that lay at his feet.

The prince scowled. "That rag!" he said. "It is nothing, and certainly it is not spectacular."

The merchant smiled slyly. "Good prince, if you step upon this rug, it will take you anywhere you wish."

The prince shook his head. "Do you think I am a fool?" he asked. "I've heard merchants' tales before."

"Allow me to show you," said the merchant, and taking the prince by the arm, he stepped upon the rug. "Now tell me, where in the world would you most like to travel?" he asked.

The prince smiled and said, "I would like to be at the palace gates where my beloved lives."

In the wink of an eye, the rug took off and traveled faster than wind to the palace gates. When they arrived, the prince stared in wonder, but before he could say a word, the merchant said "Return," and as soon as the word left his mouth, they were back in the city, beside the merchant's stall.

"I'll take it," said the prince and gave the merchant every coin he had.

Meanwhile, the second prince decided to go to a village for his gift. When he arrived, he saw a merchant staring into the bright sky with a telescope. "Sir, I am looking for the most spectacular gift in the world."

"Then you're in luck!" cried the merchant. "Look through this telescope and you will see all the wonders of the world."

The prince bent over and looked through the telescope, and there he saw his brother in the city, buying a worn, ragged rug.

"I'll take it," said the second prince, and gave the merchant all his money, for he was certain he had the most spectacular gift in the world.

The third prince was walking slowly along the country roads, humming to himself, for he believed that the countryside held the world's riches. He came to an old woman who sat on the side of the road selling apples. "Good woman," said the prince, "do you have anything for a hungry lad to eat?"

The woman looked up, smiled, and handed him a brown, wormy apple.

The prince frowned. "But I would like a red, juicy apple," he said, and so the woman bent over and searched through her baskets. At last she found a glistening ripe apple.

"How much?" asked the price.

"All your money," said the old woman.

"What madness is this?" cried the prince. "All my money for a single apple?"

"Sir," the old woman said calmly, "this is no ordinary apple. It will cure the sick of every illness. Watch."

With that she stood and took the prince by the hand and led him down the road until they came upon a sick old man who sat beside a tree, groaning with pain. The woman touched the old man's face with the apple, and a moment later he jumped up, healthy and strong.

"I am well!" he cried delightedly, and kicked his heels in the air.

The prince was so impressed he reached into his satchel and pulled out all his coins. "I'm happy to buy your apple," he said, "for certainly this is the most spectacular gift in the world."

When all three princes had returned home, each showed the others his gift, and each said, "Now here is the most spectacular gift in the world."

"Let us look through your telescope, brother," said the youngest prince, "and we shall see our beloved and her father." He bent over and looked through the telescope, and suddenly he began to tremble. "Brothers," he cried, "I see our princess and she is lying in her bed, deathly ill."

"Quickly," said the eldest prince, "climb upon my carpet and we will ride to save her."

All three princes climbed upon the rug and, whoosh, in an instant they arrived at the palace. They ran to the princess's room, and the youngest prince touched the apple to her poor, pale face. A moment later she was perfectly well.

Now all three princes turned to the king. "Tell us, sir, which of our three gifts is most spectacular. If not for this telescope, we never would have known our beloved was ill. And without this magical rug, we would not have arrived in time to save her. And without this magical apple, we would not have been able to heal your daughter. So you decide. Which of these three gifts is most spectacular?"

The king shook his head. "A most difficult decision," he said. "I don't know what to do."

At this the princess sat up in her bed and smiled, and her rosy cheeks bloomed brightly. "Father, I wish to choose my husband for myself. I love the youngest prince, and it is he I wish to wed."

And of course that was the end of that. The youngest prince and the princess married, and the two older brothers went out into the world. Each prince found a woman he loved, and they too wed. And forever afterward they shared their happiness and, also, their spectacular gifts.

The People of Chelm
Move Mountains

LONG AGO in Russia, in a village called Chelm, the people were very happy. Their village was a lovely place. They had a marketplace, a synagogue, a village square.

The people of Chelm loved their neighbors. They loved their friends. They loved their festivals and village dances. Their school was fine, the teachers wise. Their gardens bloomed in summer. In the wintertime, the people took great pleasure in the warmth of their hearths. Many children were born. They grew up, married, and bore more children.

And then, after many, many peaceful, happy years, the people of Chelm began to worry.

"Our town is too small," said Rachel.

"We need more homes for all our new people," Sarah said.

"We need a larger park for all the children," whispered Mordecai.

"Oh, the marketplace is far too small," Abraham moaned.

On and on they talked. "What will we do to solve this problem?" they cried.

Soon the people of Chelm spoke of little else but their growing problem. They gathered in the park and fretted. They wandered through the hills and talked of nothing else. Beyond the village gates, the shepherds stood upon the hills and looked down and worried too. Even they could see that soon there would be no room in the village for all of the people of Chelm.

At last, one day in early spring, the mayor gathered all the wise people of Chelm together. "Let us walk around and discuss our problem," he said. And off they walked, past the park and houses, past the school, beyond the synagogue. Soon they walked past the village boundaries and out into the fields and hills beyond.

"Ah," cried the mayor ,"here it is. Here is the solution to our problem."

"Yes," said Isaac, gently rubbing his beard, looking around. "This is the solution. Of course."

"I see," Leah said, "this field is our answer. This field will give us much more room to build and grow."

For a moment, all stood silent. They looked at the field. They observed the wildflowers growing there. They breathed in deeply and inhaled the fresh spring air.

Then they looked at the high, high mountain that stood in the very center of the wide, wonderful field. "This mountain stands in our way," said Isaac.

For another moment everyone was hushed. And then the mayor, the wisest man in all of Chelm, grinned. "Never mind!" he cried. "We shall overcome this obstacle!"

"Of course we will," said Leah.

"Yes, we'll overcome," the others cried. "But how?"

"It is easy," said the mayor. And he led the wise people back to the village square. There he announced a decree:

"We shall gather all together, tomorrow at dawn," said the mayor, "and together we shall push the tall mountain backward. Then we shall have all the space we need to expand our village."

The people cheered.

At dawn the next day all the people of Chelm gathered together and walked to the foot of the mountain. The sun began to rise. "It will be hot

today," cried Isaac. "Yes," said the people, and together they looked at the mayor.

"Now we shall lean against the mountain's side and push," said the mayor, and so they did. One by one they moved to the mountain, and they leaned against its craggy sides. They began to push. They pushed, and they pushed, and they pushed. They sang as they worked, for they began to dream of all the space they would have to build their new homes and parks and schools.

On and on they worked as the sun rose higher in the sky. The day grew hot. There was not a cloud in the sky. Not a breath of wind blew. Soon the people began sweating. They groaned and heaved and huffed.

At midday, with the sun directly overhead, the people began removing their coats and jackets. These they tossed in a big pile behind them. Then they began to push harder still. They pushed, and they pushed, and they pushed. The people of Chelm were determined, and they were strong.

Now as it happened, just then a thief from another village happened to pass by the people of Chelm who were pushing their mountain. For a moment he stopped and stared at the people. He grinned and shook his head. And then he looked, and he saw behind the people a great pile of lovely clothing. "Oh, what a price I could get for all those fine jackets and coats," he said to himself. And so, sneaking past, he moved to the pile, lifted it into his arms, and ran off with the lot.

The people pushed on. At sunset, a few people stopped their labors. "I'm exhausted," said Jacob. "Oh yes," said Sarah.

Soon the mayor called out, "Rest a while, good people." With great relief the people stopped pushing. They turned around to sit and lean and rest against the mountain's side.

Suddenly the mayor cried, "Hurrah! Hurrah for us!"

The people turned to look at him. The mayor pointed west. "Look there!" he said. "Do you see our pile of clothes?"

The people looked. They saw nothing, of course.

"Now you see," the mayor cried joyfully, "how far we have moved the mountain. We cannot even see our clothes anymore!"

At that all the people stood up, and they cheered and praised the mayor and praised God. "Oh, we have been helped in our efforts to expand our village!" they shouted.

They turned to each other and thanked each other for their mighty and determined efforts. They praised their neighbors and their friends.

And that night the people gathered together for a celebration such as they had never had before. "Our town has grown!" they sang.

All through the lovely spring night, the people of Chelm sang and danced and rejoiced at their good fortune. "We have moved a mountain!" they sang.

"Yes," said the mayor, "and we are lucky to be the people of Chelm. Let us give thanks to each and every person of our village."

And this they did.

The Lost Fishing Hook

ONCE UPON A TIME, long, long ago, two brothers lived together in Japan. The brothers were as different from each other as night from day. Hoki was generous and good and spent his days in the cool mountains, hunting for pheasants to feed the family. Hono was greedy and cruel. He spent his days by the sea, fishing for food to feed only himself. One day Hoki walked out of the mountains and, looking out to sea, he decided he would try his hand at fishing. He borrowed his brother's hook and sat at the seaside. There he fished for many hours but had no luck.

At last the sun began to set and Hoki stood to leave. Suddenly Hoki felt something grab his line. He pulled and pulled, struggling to hold onto the line, but, alas, the line snapped and the fish swam away with the hook in his mouth.

When Hoki returned home, he told his brother what had happened. Hono was furious. "You must find my fishing hook," he cried at his brother, "and you may not come back home until you have. That was a special hook." Hono hoped his brother would disappear forever.

Sad and discouraged, Hoki walked to the edge of the sea and sat down to think. "How will I ever find a lost fishhook?" he asked himself. "I will never find it, but I must," he said. At last he

30

decided to jump into the sea to search for the hook. "I do not know how to swim," he said to himself, "but I must return my brother's fishing hook."

He stood up and jumped into the cool, clear water. Down he went, down, down, down. "Surely I will drown," he gurgled, as he struggled against the water. But Hoki did not drown, for the Lord of the Tides was watching over him as he watches over all good men.

Hoki realized that he could breathe. Calming down, he let himself sink deeper and deeper, enjoying the cool embrace of the water. At last he reached the bottom of the sea and he gasped, for before him he saw an exquisite palace built of shimmering pearls and glistening shells. Sitting outside of the palace he saw, to his delight, a beautiful maiden combing her long black hair with a comb made of coral. When she looked up and saw Hoki floating toward her, she blushed and turned to run inside the palace, for she was a modest maiden and she wished to announce the arrival of this stranger to her father, the King of the Sea.

Hoki landed on the soft sand, and a moment later the maiden and the good king of the Sea greeted him, "Welcome to our watery world," said the king. Hoki was so enchanted with the beauty of the palace and the kindness of the sea creatures that he soon forgot all about his brother's fishing hook.

The Lord of the Tides and the Ladies of the Coral Reef, the beautiful maiden with her comb, and all the other members of the court were generous and gracious and welcoming. Hoki spent many days wandering through the reedy watery gardens, staring in wonder at the many creatures he had never so much as imagined. Soon he fell in love with the maiden of the coral comb, who was called the Jewel Lady. She too fell in love, for Hoki was a good, kind man, and not long afterward Hoki and the Jewel Lady married.

Three years passed in happiness, but then one day Hoki woke with a start, for he had just remembered his brother's fishing hook. "My dearest wife," he said, "I have forgotten a promise I made in Japan. I must find my brother's fishing hook and return it to him, for I told him that I would. A man must keep his promises, always."

His wife agreed. "You will need help," she said, and she went to her father to seek his advice. Soon the King of the Sea had gathered all the sea creatures together.

"We seek a fishhook lost three years ago," he said to one and all. Every creature turned and looked at every other. "Have you seen a fish-hook?" they bubbled and gurgled and murmured as the king walked through the crowds, asking the octopus, the crocodile, and every little fish. At last he came upon a sad-looking shark who sat without moving. "What's this?" asked the king, and he looked deeply into the poor, sad shark's eyes. Slowly the shark opened his mouth, and the king saw a terrible sore. He reached inside, and gently pulled. "Here is your hook," he said to Hoki.

Hoki smiled, but then, with a sad heart, he turned to his wife. "I must return to Japan to give my brother back his hook. I shall build you a palace in the countryside. I hope you will come live with me there."

The Jewel Lady embraced her husband. "I will come in a year and a day, but if I am to live on land, you must have made a palace for me, a palace as wonderful as ours below the sea. The roof must be constructed of cormorant wings. The floors must be of polished sand. Our rooms must shimmer as our walls below the sea shimmer. My husband, I am going to give birth to your son, and I wish him to live a life as gentle and sweet as our life here. Remember, one year and one day."

Hoki promised he would do his best, and with that he bade his wife

farewell. The King of the Sea turned to his son-in-law and said: "Here is a magical shell. If you need help, you must ask the shell to bring the sea to the land, and the shell will obey you. And if you tell it to send the sea back to its bed, that too shall happen."

Hoki climbed upon the back of a crocodile and rode up and up and up. At last he came to the shore where he had lost his hook so many years before. There he saw his brother Hono sitting on the beach staring out at the horizon. "Here is your hook!" Hoki cried to his brother, but Hono was furious for he had hoped and prayed that Hoki would never return.

He rushed at Hoki, drawing out an enormous silver dagger. Hoki was astonished at this, but remembering his magical shell, he looked down and whispered, "Bring up the sea." At once an enormous wave rolled up onto the beach and swept Hono into its arms.

"Return to your bed," Hoki called, and with that the wave rolled backward, taking Hono away in its strong arms, forever.

Hoki set to work at once building a palace. He worked night and day. At last, as he was placing cormorant wings upon the roof, he turned and saw his beloved, riding toward him on the back of a sea serpent. One year and one day had passed.

"The palace is not completed!" she cried. "I cannot stay with you, good husband. I will bear our child here, but then I must return to the sea."

And that is what happened. The Jewel Lady gave birth to a handsome son, and the next day the sea serpent returned to take her back to her home in the sea. She wept, and Hoki wept. They embraced one last time. Then the Jewel Lady climbed upon her serpent's back and returned to the sea.

Hoki and his son lived the rest of their days in the beautiful palace.

His son grew strong and handsome, and he was as good as his father, and as generous. As for Hoki, every evening he stood at the edge of the sea, dreaming of his wonderful wife. And below the sea, every evening she stared up at the shimmering lights above and dreamed of her husband and child. In their memories there was much joy.

Little Mouse Marries

ONCE UPON A TIME there lived a family of mice. The youngest mouse was lovely, and her parents wished to find her a suitable husband. "No one can compare to you," they said to their daughter. "Only he who is good and strong and wise and powerful is fit to marry you."

The little mouse curtsied and said in her soft, gentle voice, "Thank you, Mother and Father. You are so good to me."

And so Mr. and Mrs. Mouse set out into the world to search for a husband for their youngest daughter.

"I know!" said Mr. Mouse as he looked up at the bright blue sky. "We shall ask Sun to marry our daughter. Sun is good and kind, and he is powerful."

"Oh yes," agreed Mrs. Mouse, squinting up at the beaming Sun.

Mr. and Mrs. Mouse climbed upon a rainbow and scurried as fast as they could toward Sun. When they reached his palace, they bowed down before him and said, "Sun, please marry our daughter. You are good and strong and wise and powerful. We know you would make a fine husband for our youngest child."

Sun beamed brightly at Mr. and Mrs. Mouse. "I would be pleased to marry your daughter," he boomed. His crown gleamed. "Very happy indeed. Tell me when."

Mr. Mouse squinted and leaned close to Mrs.

Mouse, but just as he was about to speak, he heard a roaring thunderclap. A black cloud appeared and blotted out Sun's bright rays. "Hmm," said Mr. Mouse. "I wonder if Sun is truly the most powerful being on earth."

Mrs. Mouse looked at Sun, who now appeared not as bright as he had been. "Tell me," she said, "are you the most powerful being on earth?"

Sun glinted and frowned. "No," he whispered, "I am not. Rain is more powerful than I, I'm afraid. When he comes, I must close my eyes and I do not glow so brightly."

Just then Rain swept past the rainbow, furious and fast. He galloped across the sky, and Sun disappeared.

"Rain!" cried Mr. Mouse, staring at the powerful being. "Rain, please. We wish you to marry our daughter, the lovely Little Mouse."

Thunder clapped and lightning flashed across the sky as Rain looked down at Mr. and Mrs. Mouse. "I'd be happy to marry your Little Mouse," he said in a light patter, but he did not finish his sentence, for just then gusty Wind came along and swept Rain far away.

"Ahh," cried Mr. Mouse as he held onto his hat. "Wind, of course! You are powerful and good and strong and very wise, and it is you who drives Rain hither and yon."

"That is I," breathed Wind, letting forth a great gush of himself and nearly blowing Mr. and Mrs. Mouse off the rainbow.

"Will you marry our daughter, Little Mouse?" asked Mrs. Mouse. "We wish her to marry the most powerful being on earth."

"Oooff," gasped Wind. "I am afraid you are mistaken if you think I am most powerful." He huffed and puffed, and all the clouds began to dance around him. Soon, in the distance, Mr. and Mrs. Mouse saw Sun winking at them.

"You see," said Wind, "I am quite powerful, and I am good, but no matter how I try, I cannot blow Mountain away. See him standing there?

Just watch." And with that Wind blew and blew and the clouds danced faster still. But Mountain stood firmly in place.

"Thank you so much," said Mr. and Mrs. Mouse. They scampered down the rainbow and across the wide fields. Standing at Mountain's great, craggy foot, they looked up and said, "Mountain, will you marry our daughter, Little Mouse? She is a most wonderful creature, and we wish her husband to be the most powerful and wise being on earth."

Mountain stood stock still and said nothing for many moments. At last his voice came, almost as an echo. "I would love to marry your daughter," he said, "but I am not so powerful as you think. Look there."

Mr. and Mrs. Mouse turned and saw a great Bull approaching Mountain's foot.

"Bull comes to me every evening. He rests his head against my sides. Oh, those horns of his, just look at them," sighed Mountain. "They are so strong and powerful that when he shakes his head against me, great chunks of my skin break and fall off."

"Surely you can stop him," said Mr. Mouse.

"No, I am afraid I cannot," said Mountain. "So you see, Bull is more powerful than I."

Mr. and Mrs. Mouse nodded. They turned and walked across the field to greet great Bull. Overhead the stars began to twinkle in the evening sky. "What a fine evening to meet a bridegroom, isn't it, Mrs. Mouse?"

"Oh yes, husband. A fine evening indeed!"

With that they stopped in front of Bull and looked up into his eyes. "Oh, great Bull, Mountain has sent us to you, for he says you are the most powerful being on earth. With deep respect, we ask you to marry our daughter, Little Mouse."

Bull snorted and looked down at the couple. "I am honored," he roared, "and I would gladly marry Little Mouse. But I'm afraid Mountain is wrong. The most powerful being on earth is Rope. He is the creature you see here, wrapped around my neck. If he pulls left, I must move left. If he pulls right, I must move right. I am powerless before powerful Rope."

"Thank you so much," squeaked Mrs. Mouse, and she looked at Rope and smiled her widest smile. "Rope, would you be my daughter's husband? According to Sun and Rain and Wind and Mountain and Bull, it is you who are the most powerful being on earth."

"I would love to marry Little Mouse," cried Rope, and in his joy, he swung himself this way and that. The stars above seemed to twinkle brighter still.

Mrs. Mouse said happily, "Well, then, that is settled, dear husband."

Suddenly Rope stopped swinging and said sadly: "I am afraid there is a creature who is more powerful than I. It is Mouse, who lives in the shed where I hang my head each night. He comes and gnaws and tears at me. No matter how hard I try, I can do nothing to stop him."

Mrs. Mouse smiled at Rope. "I see," she said, and Mr. Mouse said, "I see, too."

They went quickly to the cowshed and there they found the powerful Mouse. He lay among a pile of straw, biding his time.

"Will you marry our daughter, Little Mouse?" asked Mr. Mouse. "Everyone agrees that you are the most powerful being on earth."

"I would be most pleased to marry your daughter," said Mouse.

And the very next day Mouse and Little Mouse were married, and they lived afterward in great happiness.

Stanford and Amelia, Pig and Goose

PART ONE

ONCE UPON A TIME, near the banks of a long, winding river, there lived a pleasant pig family. For years the family lived in peace, feasting upon the flowers that bloomed in abundance in their fields.

Sometimes the family grew tired of their flowers. Then they organized a party, and together they trudged steadily over the hills and feasted on the food in the farmers' fields. "Oh, celebrations and feasts!" they cried, as they munched and munched until they could not eat another bite. Then together they returned to the bank of the river, and all night long they sang and danced.

These holidays were rare, but always gave great pleasure. Sometimes on a festive occasion, the family worked together all day long to make a glorious pool. Then they dived in and slipped and slid and rolled and frolicked, miring themselves in the delightful mud they made.

Most of the time, of course, the family was well organized and proper, clean, and careful to take care of their land and to complete daily tasks. They were proud and knew the value of their property; they loved their riverbank. They loved their flowers. They loved the dazzling sunsets and the red dawns. And life went on.

Most of the pigs were happy, but one was not. Stanford was the youngest boar, a boar with a generous heart. He spent a good deal of his time worrying and wandering. Sometimes he would travel off, alone, into the fields across the river and over the mountains. There he listened to others' stories. He heard others talk. He listened hard. Then hurrying on his sturdy legs, he returned home to tell his family the rumors he'd heard.

"Just listen," he would say, "what they say about us on the far side of the hills. It is quite terrible."

"What is it now?" his father asked, annoyed by his son's worrisome nature.

"They say we're filthy," Stanford said. "I've heard them say we're dirty, disgusting creatures, Father. I've heard them talk . . . "

"So much for intelligence," his father sighed. "What do others know anyway?" Brigitte added. "They don't know us!"

"But I hear them complain," Stanford went on. "They say we squeal!"

"Understand," Maria said with utmost calm, "some have no ear for music. Some are not so sensitive as we." And Stanford's mother came to him and tried to calm his fears. At that Stanford began to shiver.

"Listen!" he cried, "I just remembered something terrible I heard. Someone said something about mother's ear."

"A sow's ear!" laughed Mortimer, and he rolled on the ground and shook with pleasure. "It's one of those tales you hear."

"But listen," Stanford said, "they talked about my mother's ears and making silk purses of them!"

The others laughed and teased Stanford about his worries. And then, seeing that it was no use to comfort their troubled young brother, they went on singing and enjoying life on their riverbank.

But Stanford could not cease worrying. "They're coming to get us," he told his family. "They say that hunting pigs is a favorite pastime. They say they mean to catch us and snap off our tails."

At this the pigs broke into laughter again. They turned and snapped

each other's tails and blew into each other's ears. "Like this?" they laughed. "Like that?"

"I'm going to tell them to stop!" Stanford said. "I'm going to tell them who we are and what we do and I will stop these rumors. Listen to me! Listen now!" he cried, and off he stomped.

He flopped upon the riverbank and wondered about what he could possibly do to stop the stories spreading near and far.

"All the stories I have heard," Stanford said to himself. "No one loves us. No one understands who we are and what we do and why!" On and on he wailed and moaned. He remembered insults he had heard. "Unlucky . . . we're unlucky!" he wept, "When we sit beside a boat. And dirty! And beastly! Why do they despise us so? And why does no one understand me or listen to me?"

He looked across the field and watched his family munching merrily upon the flowers. But he could not summon up his appetite. He felt far too sad.

As Stanford lay upon the riverbank, weeping and worrying, he heard a flutter in the reeds. When he turned he saw an elegant, white-feathered gosling floating peacefully upon the glistening river. She floated toward him. "Why are you moaning?" she asked softly. She had listened to Stanford's cries, and they broke her heart.

"No one loves me," Stanford said. "Out there they say they mean to catch us and to take our ears, our tails, our home. And here," he nodded toward his family, "they laugh at me. They love their flowers more than they love me!"

The gosling sat very still and listened while Stanford recounted his tales. She did not laugh, for she could see that he was very sad. And she could see he was as honest as the day. "You are telling the truth," she said. "I see that you are."

"Why would I lie!" he cried. "Why would I invent stories about my own family?"

"I know you would not," said Amelia, for that was the young gosling's name.

At that Stanford stopped moaning. He turned to look at Amelia. No one had ever believed him. This was so pleasurable he could not speak. And when he looked closely, he gasped, for the sunlight shone upon her now. Her feathers glistened like a precious jewel, and Stanford felt his heart swelling to twice its size.

"What lovely feathers," he sighed. "Oh, you are beautiful. Everyone must love a creature as beautiful as you!"

"Now Stanford," said Amelia, looking down, "just look, right here. Look in the river's mirror. You're handsome as can be!"

"I am?" he asked, and he leaned to look. He smiled. "Well, I look like the pig that I am," he said. "You only think me handsome because you do not despise me."

"I could never despise someone as clean and proud as you," said Amelia. She flapped her wings, for she felt her heart growing soft. And when Stanford and Amelia looked at each other again, they knew that they were in love.

PART TWO

Y OU ARE my dearest friend," Stanford said to his beloved Amelia, but just at that moment, they heard a pop and a shriek coming from the farthest field. They turned to look and saw the farmers rushing from their truck, chasing Stanford's family, every one. The farmers carried nets and guns, and Stanford's family ran, hither and yon. They cried out for help.

At once Stanford began to run toward them. Amelia pecked his back and pulled at his skin. "Stop, Stanford," she cried. "Be still! Be still!"

"I must go to my family," he screamed. "Amelia, let me go."

Amelia held fast. And Stanford, who had not the heart to leave his beloved, stopped and watched. They saw the farmers catch Stanford's family, one by one. They swept their nets down over them; they caught them by the tails; they held their snouts. And they hurled them, one by one, into the back of their blue pickup truck.

"Oh, Stanford," cried Amelia, "please don't run away. Don't leave me, please. I have fallen quite in love with you."

Stanford turned and looked at Amelia. His heart, which was quite large and very soft, began to ache. "I love you too," he said softly, "but I must go . . ." He turned to leave. But he could not move. Without looking back at her, he said, "Amelia, I'll never forget you." Then pulling hard, he ran off toward the field. And as he ran, his heart swelled so large he thought that any minute it would break.

Stanford reached the edge of the field, and just as he plunged toward the farmers, he heard the roar of an engine, the whir of wheels. Dust flew into his eyes, and in the next instant, the truck and all his family were gone.

Stanford let out a piercing wail and flopped onto the ground and wept until he thought his heart would crack in two. "Brigitte," he moaned.

"Maria, Mother, Uncle Ralph, Gordy, Patrice, Paulette . . ." They were gone, every one. And Stanford lay in his field of flowers all alone, weeping and wailing.

The weather changed abruptly the next day. The chill winds blew in from the north and howled and whistled at the poor pig lying very still in his field. The wind whipped his back and chafed his skin, but Stanford would not move. He barely felt the pain, for he was so sad.

"I'm so alone, and this is all so terrible!" he wailed. And then, suddenly, he stopped wailing, for he heard a flap and a flutter, and when he looked up he saw, standing beside him, his beloved Amelia.

"Come with my family, Stanford," she said. "We will leave this place and go to another. I want you to be with me in our winter home. Please come away, now."

"Where is your winter home?" he asked. When he looked at Amelia, once again his heart swelled and he felt happy and peaceful and loved. She was his true friend. "Amelia, where are you traveling?"

"That way," Amelia said. She pointed south. "Across the river, over valleys and mountains and hills and streams. Past many lands. A long, long way away," she said.

"But why are you leaving?" Stanford asked, as she wiped a tear from his snout.

"It grows chilly here," said Amelia, "and we wish to spend the winter warm. We have two homes, you see. We like to see the whole wide world."

"I must not lose you," Stanford wept. "I've lost everyone else."

"Then you'll come!" cried Amelia, delighted at the thought of being always with her dear friend.

"How will I go?" he asked. "You say it is so far. These legs are strong and sturdy, but they cannot walk so many miles."

"Hush, Stanford," Amelia said. "Sometimes you talk too much. Come with me." He did, but as they walked, Stanford talked, and he talked, and he talked.

"Amelia, I am a pig and you are a gosling, and you can fly, and I am here, stuck to the earth, stuck in this field, and I love you but you are not alone, and you are loved, and I am not, I have no family."

On and on he went, starting again on the woes of his life, on the stories people told, on rumors. "Oh, Amelia, if you only knew how terrible it is, the way they say we are ugly and filthy beasts, the way they talk about us, and the way I am alone right here, without my family, and about to lose my love."

"Hush now!" said Amelia. "My family has a plan." Stanford looked at her, opening his wide eyes still wider. "What sort of plan?" he asked.

"Quiet now and listen to what my father tells us," Amelia said. And she took him to her family.

The geese were gathered together, wading idly by the river's edge, conferring quietly. Stanford tried to hear what they were saying, but their voices were so quiet, and the wind blew so loudly, that he could not hear their words. Once again he began to worry. "Amelia," he said to his friend, "do they hate me too?"

"Heavens no, my friend, be quiet. Please!"

Stanford held his peace and sat and waited while the geese discussed the poor pig's plight.

At last Amelia's father turned to him. "Now take this stick, Stanford," he said, "and hold it tightly in your mouth."

"But sir . . ." Stanford began.

"Quiet!" said Amelia's father. "Listen to us. You will hold this stick in your mouth, and Amelia and I will carry you across the river and over valleys and mountains and streams, and we will fly over many lands and bring you with us to our winter home. There you and Amelia will be together, and at peace."

Stanford's heart swelled with happiness. "I can't believe how lucky . . ."

"Yes, we are," Amelia said. "Few have such true friends as we have."

And with that Stanford took the stick in his mouth and clamped down hard. In the next moment, he and Amelia and her family were flying high over the wide river.

On and on they flew. Stanford's mouth ached, but he barely felt the pain, for watching his beloved take her graceful turns, he could think of no words to describe the way he felt for her. "Love," he said to himself, but that was not enough.

And then, suddenly, he heard beneath him people shouting and crying. "Look at that," they cried, "a flying pig! Absurd! Ridiculous! The filthy beast." They laughed and pointed.

Amelia turned and saw her friend's face flush.

"Stanford," she cautioned, "do not open your mouth," and he clamped down harder on the stick, and tears flowed from his eyes.

And then Amelia cried out, as loudly as she could, and all the people stared up in wonder. "You do not know what you see! You speak without knowledge. If only you would learn to listen, you too could fly!"

And on they flew to their new home. There Stanford and Amelia lived happily ever after.

The Clever Girl

ONCE UPON A TIME there lived a poor farmer who had one trusted treasure. This was his daughter, Hannah. One day the farmer became involved in a dispute over a cow with his neighbor. Because they could not agree on a solution, the two men traveled to the palace to seek the magistrate's help.

The magistrate was a kind man, but he was young and inexperienced. He listened carefully to both sides of the story. At last he said: "Instead of deciding the case, I will put a riddle to you. The man who answers best shall win the dispute. Do you agree to this?"

The two men nodded, certain that they could answer whatever question the magistrate might pose.

Then the magistrate asked: "Tell me this. What is the swiftest thing in the world? What is the sweetest thing? And what is the richest? Bring me your answers tomorrow."

Back home, the neighbor asked his wife to help him solve the riddle. "Easy," she said as she scooped porridge into a bowl. "Our gray mare is the swiftest thing in the world, for no one ever passes us on the road. As for the sweetest thing, that is our honey. And nothing can be richer than our chest full of gold that I've been saving these many years."

The farmer, in his turn, told his daughter of the magistrate's riddle.

Hannah sat down beside him and touched his hand. "Please, father, let me help," she said, for she wished nothing more than her father's happiness. When the farmer told her the three questions, she smiled. "That's easy," she said, and she explained to her father how to answer the riddle.

The next day the two men returned to the magistrate to answer the riddle. First the neighbor offered his answers. Then the farmer said, "I humbly answer, sir. The swiftest thing in all the world is thought, for thought can run any distance in the twinkling of an eye. The sweetest thing is sleep, for when one is tired, nothing is sweeter. The richest thing is the earth, for it provides us with all our riches."

The magistrate was impressed. "Tell me, good man, how did you know these answers?" The farmer proudly told the magistrate of his intelligent, clever daughter.

The magistrate listened thoughtfully and said, "I would like to make another test of your daughter's cleverness." He sent for ten eggs, and these he gave to the farmer. "Take these eggs to Hannah and tell her to have them hatched by tomorrow."

The farmer dashed home and gave the eggs to Hannah. She laughed. "Father, take a handful of millet and return to the magistrate at once. Say to him, 'My daughter sends you this millet and says that if you plant, grow, and harvest it by tomorrow, she will bring you the chicks.'"

When the magistrate heard Hannah's answer, he laughed heartily. "Clever girl she is. I would like to meet her, but one more test. Tell her she must come to me, but she must come neither by day nor by night, neither riding nor walking, neither dressed nor undressed."

Once again the farmer ran home to tell his daughter of the magistrate's request. Hannah waited until dawn, then, when night was past but day not yet begun, she wrapped herself in fish netting, threw one leg over a goat's back and the other she kept on the ground. And she traveled in this way to the magistrate's home.

When she arrived she cried out, "Sir, I am here, neither riding nor walking, neither dressed nor undressed, neither by day nor by night."

The magistrate was so taken by Hannah's cleverness and so pleased with her wit that he proposed marriage to her at once, and in a short time they were wed.

"Understand, dear Hannah," said the magistrate on their wedding day, "you are not to use that cleverness of yours at my expense. You must not interfere in my cases. And if you ever give advice to anyone who comes to me for a judgment, I will turn you out of my house and send you back to your father."

"I promise you that," said Hannah, "but I ask you one promise in return. If you ever choose to send me away, allow me to take with me the one thing that I most treasure."

The magistrate readily promised, for he was not a selfish man. And for a long time the magistrate and Hannah lived together happily.

Then one day two farmers came to the magistrate hoping he might settle a dispute. One of the farmers owned a mare that had foaled in the marketplace. The colt had run beneath the wagon of the other farmer. Now the owner of the wagon claimed the colt as his own.

The magistrate was preoccupied with other matters and was not listening closely. "The man who found the colt under his wagon is the true owner," he said carelessly.

As the owner of the mare was leaving the palace, he met up with Hannah who was wandering in the palace garden. The farmer looked so sad that Hannah could not help herself. "What is wrong, good man?" she asked. And the farmer told his tale.

Saddened by her husband's decision, Hannah said, "Come back this afternoon, good sir. Bring with you a fishing net and stretch it across the road outside the garden gate. When the magistrate sees you, he will ask how you expect to catch fish on a dusty road. You must tell him it is just as easy to catch fish in a road as it is for a wagon to foal. In this way he shall see the injustice of his decision."

That afternoon the farmer returned to the magistrate's home. He stretched his fishing net across the road. When the magistrate saw him, he shouted, "What's this foolishness? How do you expect to catch any fish on a dusty road?"

And when the magistrate heard the farmer's answer, he frowned and said: "My decision was wrong. The colt belongs to the owner of the mare, of course." The farmer, dancing with delight, cried, "Ah, your wife is a very fine woman!"

When the magistrate heard this, he grew furious with Hannah. He ran to her and said, "You have broken your promise to me. Home you must go, this very day."

Hannah looked steadily at her husband. "You are right," she said sadly, "but I ask you one favor. Share one last supper with me. We have been happy together, and I wish to part as friends."

The magistrate could not say no, for he truly loved Hannah. That night the two sat down together, and to the magistrate's delight, before him was spread a meal of all his favorite dishes. He ate and he ate until at last, so full he could not move, he fell fast asleep in his chair.

Quickly Hannah rose from the table. Without waking her husband, she had him carried out to her carriage.

The next morning the magistrate opened his eyes and saw, to his amazement, that he lay in a bed in Hannah's father's cottage. "What's this?" he roared.

"My dear husband," said Hannah gently, coming to his bedside, "you told me I might take the one thing I liked best in your house. I took you. It is you I most treasure."

In the next moment the magistrate was laughing long and loud, for Hannah had again outwitted him. "Hannah, I have been a fool. Please come home with me." And he got down on his knees and begged for her forgiveness.

Afterward, whenever the magistrate had to make a difficult decision, he announced to one and all, "We shall consult my wife, for she is a clever woman, and very wise."

Valley of the Huanacos

LONG AGO in South America the Gentle People lived in perfect harmony and happiness among the animals and birds, flowers and trees. The Gentle People were kind, graceful, and beautiful. And they had a special talent as well. They could change the many brightly colored flowers that grew in abundance into living birds. The bright blue skies were filled with birds. Scissortails darted to and fro, flashing their tails. Bright red ovenbirds sang to glossy-coated violet cowbirds. Lapwings filled the air with song.

The land was wonderful. The flowers smelled sweeter than flowers anywhere else in the world. The sun never shone too brightly. The winds never blew harshly. The Prince of the Gentle People was good and wise; he loved his people and his land and the world they inhabited.

The people often gathered together to praise their prince and his goodness. They brought with them precious stones, and these the prince tossed to the children. The Gentle People, you see, loved things for their beauty alone. At the gatherings, the birds and animals sang and danced with the people. And on those days, each person had one wish granted, no matter what it was.

There was but one rule, and it was this: The prince forbade the Gentle People to travel too far north. North, the prince explained, where the Southern Cross no longer glistened overhead, there was a deep, dark forest filled with evil men. The Gentle People must not go there.

Alas, one day a young man named Capa looked up in the sky and saw a strange bird such as he had never before seen. The creature's breast was green and blue and gold. His long tail was as white as ivory. Capa called to the bird. "Come here, creature, and let me look at you."

To his surprise, the bird flew quickly away.

That is strange, he said to himself. The birds in this land were friends to the Gentle People. I must find this bird and take him to our prince. He is so different from the birds I know.

And so Capa followed the bird's path as he winged northward. On and on he flew, and Capa followed, always looking up. "How odd that he will not let me touch him and hold him," Capa said as he traveled. "How very odd." For, you see, the Gentle People did not know fear.

At last Capa came to the edge of the dark, deep forest. When he looked up, he no longer saw the Southern Cross. The bird flew on, still moving north. For a moment Capa hesitated, but he longed to know this bird. And so he walked on, into the forest.

At last he came to a clearing and before him he saw men with evil eyes. They sat in a clearing, eating the flesh of animals. They wore skins of animals around their bodies.

Capa stared in wonder at these strange people. He had never known a man to hurt an animal.

When the men saw Capa, they surrounded him. Quickly they grabbed his robes of silver and gold thread from him. They reached into his sleeves and drew out precious stones. And then, to Capa's amazement, the men began to fight with each other. They ripped the robe apart. They dropped the rubies and emeralds and gold as they tried to take these from each other.

While the people fought among themselves, Capa fled. He ran all the way home to his people. He went directly to the prince to tell his tale.

When the prince heard Capa's story, he grew very sad. "You have been to the land where greed and selfishness and hatred live," he said. "Now the evil men will not rest until they have found us. They wish to bring their sorrows to all."

The prince called the Gentle People all together. He told them what Capa had seen. "Now we have but two choices," said the prince. "I can provide you arms and teach you how to fight. When the evil men come, we can do battle."

The people listened and grew sad. The birds stopped singing, and the animals no longer danced. Even the fragrant flowers began to droop.

"I caution you," the prince said, "if you learn to fight, you will turn on each other and bring death to our own people. You will turn against our animals, and they will turn against you. You will begin to hide your emeralds and rubies, your gold and your silver. You will bury your belongings and keep them to yourself. That is what will happen if I arm you and teach you to fight."

The Gentle People looked at each other and they knew what they must do. "We will leave this place, then," they said. "We would rather go far, far away than learn to do evil."

When the people heard the men tramping through the forest toward them, the prince called to them to follow him. Off they went, the Gentle People and their animals and birds.

After many days they came to a deep green valley where a bright blue river ran swiftly.

"Now people, listen," said the prince, and the people gathered around him. "The men are coming after us, and so I am going to change you into animals. I will call you huanacos. You will wear red and white, and gold and silver too, and you will always be a friend to every bird and animal."

And so the prince changed his people into huanacos, and then he changed himself into the tallest and handsomest huanaco of all. He climbed onto a tall rock to watch over his people, and there he remained until, one day, he died.

The other huanacos laid the prince's bones in their valley. The very next day, a flower as blue as the sky sprouted and blossomed where once the bones had lain. Its petals were gold-tipped and its scent was fragrant. Ever afterward, whenever a huanaco died, the others buried his bones in the valley. Every huanaco bone transformed itself into a fragrant blue flower.

To this day, they say, the huanacos live in peace in the valley the people call Valley of the Gallegos in southern Patagonia. The people say that when the last huanaco dies, the evil men will disappear from the earth. And on that day every flower will bend toward its neighbor, and the Gentle People will once again have their land. Kindness and gentleness, goodness and generosity, peace and goodwill will reign forever.

The Thirsty Tree

ONCE UPON A TIME four men were walking near a dam. They came upon a leaning tree. Its long, spindly branches stretched far out over the water.

"A tree ought to stand tall and upright," said the first man. "It is sad to see a tree weeping this way."

They all agreed.

"Aha!" said the second man. "I think I know what the problem is."

They all gathered around to listen.

"The tree must be terribly thirsty," said the second man.

"It is leaning down to try to take a drink!" cried the third.

"Yes, yes," they all agreed.

Now the men felt sorry for the poor thirsty tree and decided they must help it out. They would pull the branches down until they touched the water. In this way the tree could have a drink and would weep no longer.

They jumped and leaped, trying to reach the branches. But the tree was very tall and not one of the men could reach even the lowest branch.

They sat down in a circle to think over the problem.

After a long while, the first man stood up and said: "I know what we shall do. We'll make a human rope and pull a branch down to the water!"

"Good plan!" they agreed.

And so the first man climbed the tree and crawled out to the end of one branch. He held on with his hands and let his legs swing down. The

second man reached up and grabbed the first man's legs. Then the third man reached up and held tightly to the second man's legs. The fourth man stood on shore, ready to pull on the third man's legs.

"Now," said the fourth man, "when I give a good pull, the branch will come down. It will reach the water and have a drink."

"Wait!" cried the first man, for he felt quite a strain, as you may well imagine. It isn't easy holding two men from your legs. "I forgot to spit on my hands to keep a good grip." And he let go of the branch to spit on his hands.

SPLASH, all three men fell into the water. Up they came, bubbling and gurgling. "I suppose we ought to have remembered to spit on our hands before we climbed," said the first man.

"Yes, that would have been a good idea," said the second.

They all agreed, but alas, they were too wet and miserable to try again, and so they shook their heads and apologized to the tree and set off for home to dry themselves and rest.

And the tree did not get a drink after all.

The Boy Who Went to the North Wind

ONCE UPON A TIME an old widow sent her only son out to the barn to fetch some meal. Just as the lad was walking out of the barn with it, the North Wind blew up fierce and wild. Huffing and puffing, the North Wind caught up the meal from the lad's arms, and off it blew, far, far away.

The lad, who was a hearty boy and never worried much, turned around and walked back into the barn. Once more he walked outside, carrying his bowl of fresh meal. Again the North Wind came along, and with a huff and a puff, it carried off the second bowlful.

The lad shrugged and returned to the barn a third time. Once more the North Wind made off with the meal.

Now the lad stomped his feet and his face grew bright red. He looked up at the sky, for he had grown angry with the North Wind for his tricks. "I'll go off and speak to him about his thievery," he said to himself. And so he did.

The way to the North Wind's home was long and wearying. The lad walked and walked, and finally, after the sun had set and the moon began to rise, he came to the house of the North Wind.

"Good evening, North Wind," he said.

"Good evening," heaved the North Wind. "What do you want?"

The lad politely asked the North Wind if he might return the stolen meal. He explained that his poor mother was weak and ill, and that the family was very poor. The North Wind remained very still, listening hard.

The boy went on. "If you take away our meal," he said, "we will surely starve, for we have no money to buy more."

At last the North Wind answered the lad. "I do not have your meal," said he, "but since you seem to be in need and you have traveled so far, I will reward you for your trouble. I shall give you a cloth that will fetch you any food you wish. All you have to do is say, 'Cloth, spread yourself,' and the cloth will serve up delicious dishes to eat."

The lad was pleased with this gift. He thanked the North Wind and set off for his long journey home. At last he grew weary, and spotted an inn at the side of the road. "I shall rest here tonight," he said, and walked inside.

He arrived just as the guests were sitting down to eat their supper. "Welcome," said the innkeeper, "but I'm afraid we do not have enough food to share with you."

"Never mind that," said the lad, and he lay his cloth upon the table and grinned. "Cloth, spread yourself!" A moment later, the table was filled with such a feast as you have never seen before. Everyone clapped and cheered and praised the lad.

But that night, when everyone was fast asleep, the innkeeper sneaked into the boy's room and stole the magical cloth. He replaced it with an ordinary cloth.

Next morning the lad set off, carrying with him his cloth. When he returned home, he told his mother all about his meeting with the North Wind. Then he spread out the cloth and said, "Cloth, spread yourself!"

Nothing happened.

The lad's mother just shook her head, but the boy smiled and said, "I must return to the North Wind and discover what has happened to the cloth. I am sure he did not mean to cheat us." And off he went.

He arrived at the North Wind's house late in the day. "Please, North Wind," said the lad, "this cloth is worth nothing, for it worked only once. I'd like my meal back."

The North Wind exhaled. "I told you, I have no meal. But I see that you have again traveled far," he said kindly. "For your trouble, I shall give you the ram that stands over there in the pen. This is a special ram. He produces gold coins from his mouth as soon as you say, 'Ram, make money!'"

The boy was pleased with this. Off he went once more, leading the ram behind him.

He grew very tired. Once again he stopped at the inn at the side of the road. When the boy saw all the people gathered there, he could not help but show off his good fortune.

The people gasped as they watched the ram produce gold coins. They applauded and cheered the young lad and his magical ram.

That night the innkeeper once more sneaked into the lad's room and exchanged his ordinary ram for the ram that made the gold coins.

In the morning the lad hastened home to his mother, leading the ram behind him. "Watch this, Mother," he said delightedly. "Ram, make money!" he cried.

The ram stood very still and stared at the lad. "Ram, make money," the boy repeated.

Alas, the ram produced nothing at all.

And so again the lad hastened to the home of the North Wind. This time he demanded his meal.

"I do not have any meal," sighed the North Wind, "and all I have to give you now is this old wooden stick. Now, if you say to this stick, 'Stick, lay on,' it will flap and flail and fly after anyone you wish, and it will not stop until you say, 'Stop, stick, stop now.'"

The lad went off, carrying his magical stick. Once again he stopped at the inn. When he saw the innkeeper, he squinted his eyes, for you see, by this time, he had grown suspicious.

That night the lad lay in his bed, but he did not fall asleep. Instead, he closed his eyes and pretended to snore. Now the landlord had spied the stick, and he thought it must be magical. And so, when he heard the lad's snoring begin, he sneaked into his room. He tiptoed to the corner and reached for the stick, but just as he was about to take it, the boy sat up on his bed and cried, "Stick, lay on."

The stick began to flail and fly about the ears of the startled innkeeper. Now the stick began to chase the man around the table, under the bed, beneath tables and chairs. The stick flew after him, twirling and twisting, moving faster and faster.

"Your stick means to hurt me!" cried the innkeeper. "Stop it!" But the boy sat very still upon his bed and watched as the stick chased the innkeeper. He moved fast, but the stick chased him still.

"Stop your stick!" cried the innkeeper, who was huffing and puffing.

"What will you do for me?" asked the lad.

"I will give back your cloth, and your ram, too," said the innkeeper. Now his face was red and sweat poured from his forehead. "Please stop your stick!" he sputtered as he jumped on the bed.

"Stop, stick, stop now," said the boy, and the stick fell to the ground and lay at his feet.

At once the innkeeper returned the North Wind's gifts to the boy, and he went back home, singing all the way, eager to share his good fortune with his poor old mother.

The Heinzelmannchen

ONCE UPON A TIME, long ago in the city of Cologne, there lived thousands of little creatures. They were the Heinzelmannchen, and they were kind and helpful servants. The Heinzelmannchen loved to help all the busy housewives with their mending and chores, and they also helped craftsmen and weavers and potters and woodsmen. There was no work the Heinzelmannchen would not do.

Everyone knew they were there, but no one ever saw them. They came in the middle of the night, silent and unseen, and at once they set to work. In the dark night they finished everyone's unfinished chores, and in the morning when the people woke, they found their work complete. The housewives and servants had an easy life in those days, for their work was always done, and always done well.

The Heinzelmannchen finished the last of the weaving; they polished the silver and waxed the floors. They sawed and chopped, cleaned and cooked. If the cook left her pot on the stove, they cut up more carrots and potatoes and added these to the pot. Then they stirred and stewed and finished the cooking. They kneaded the baker's bread and cut the leather-maker's leather and shined and stitched the cobbler's shoes. They weeded the gardens, polished the brass, washed the clothes.

Oh, the people loved the Heinzelmannchen!

The Heinzelmannchen loved weddings, and it was then they made their presence especially known. In the middle of the night they scampered from house to house, gathering gifts from one house and taking these to the brides' homes. "Where did my favorite lamp go now?" a man would ask in the morning. He might blame someone else for the theft.

But the Heinzelmannchen never took a thing from the kind and generous people. They were always rewarded for their goodness. To them, the Heinzelmannchen brought fine gifts.

Still, as we've said, no one ever saw the Heinzelmannchen. They were invisible by day, and though people sometimes stayed awake all night to catch one of the creatures, the Heinzelmannchen always knew. On those nights they would stay away.

People talked, of course. They speculated. "They must be white-haired," people said. "Surely they are wizened, with sturdy hands and feet and strong muscles," others mused. "They work so hard, their hands must be wrinkled and hard."

The Heinzelmannchen loved one tailor especially well. Every night he put away his sewing, and at dawn his work was done. His business prospered and grew, for his work was the finest in all the land, thanks to the Heinzelmannchen.

When the tailor married, his wife was so amazed at the work that she longed to know exactly who the Heinzelmannchen were. She asked everyone — the butcher, the baker, the priest, and even passersby. They only said, "We know no more than you."

The tailor begged and begged his wife not to ask. "We are blessed. We should be grateful. That is all," he said.

So the woman went to see the priest. "They are heathen creatures," said the priest, "that is all." You see, the priest believed his housekeeper did all the work herself, and she, good woman though she was, had not the heart to tell him that she never could, all by herself, bring such a bright shine to all the candlesticks, mend all of his clothes, cook all of his meals, sweep his floors and dust his furniture, and keep his house so fine.

But the tailor's wife was determined, and at last she could bear the mystery no longer. She took to stealing out of bed at night and going quietly downstairs to see if she might catch a glimpse of the little people. She settled down upon the kitchen floor to watch and wait.

Each dawn she woke cold and cross, for the Heinzelmannchen, as we've said, always knew if someone watched, and those nights they did not come to the tailor's house.

At last one morning the woman had a grand idea. She never told a soul about her plan, which is very sad indeed, for if she had she might have been warned.

That night, while everyone slept, the tailor's wife slipped down to the kitchen and took a jar of dried peas from the shelf. This she carried up the stairs with her, and as she walked, she put a handful of peas upon each step, leaving a trail behind her. At the top she closed the can and returned to bed.

"Ahh," she breathed deeply. "Now one of them is bound to trip and fall downstairs and hurt himself, and in the morning he will be there when I wake." Then she fell fast asleep.

When the Heinzelmannchen came that night and saw the mess upon the steps, they stared in disbelief. "How could the tailor be so lazy as to leave his peas upon the stairs?" they asked. "How could he be so cruel as to try to trick us!"

At last they grew quite furious, and so, without doing a stitch of work, the little people slipped out of the house.

In the morning the tailor's wife woke and ran to the stairs, filled with pleasure at the thought that at last she would catch the little creatures. To her dismay, she saw that not a single pea had been disturbed, and not one stitch of work was done. And the little people never came again to the good tailor's house.

The woman grumbled and groaned and moped. From that day on she had to clean and polish, sweep and dust. She had to do all the chores that the little people had once done for her. And her husband, who was now overworked and tired of his wife's nagging, grew bitter and sad.

Alas, the tailor's wife was not the only person in Cologne who tried to trick the little people. As time went on, more and more people tried to trick them, and so the Heinzelmannchen visited fewer and fewer houses in Cologne, for they feared the people's strange tricks.

At last one day the people in the city heard a sound outside their doors. It was drumming they heard, tap tap tap tap. The Heinzelmannchen were outside, in broad daylight, marching along playing pipes and drums. The people called out, "Come, come look! The Heinzelmannchen march!" The people ran to their doors and windows.

Alas, those who had been too curious could not see the Heinzelmannchen, and sad to say, that meant no one could see them, but everyone heard their music, and everyone heard the marching of their tiny feet on the cobblestones.

The music faded as the little people passed through the city's gates. At last no one could hear a sound.

No one knows where the Heinzelmannchen went or where they live now, but everyone knows that the people of Cologne were never so happy again as they had been in the days when the Heinzelmannchen lived amongst them.

The Moon Girl

ONCE UPON A TIME, a poor farmer's wife gave birth to a beautiful girl. The moment the girl was born, the wife turned to her husband and said, "Lungelo, never take our little one into the sunlight, for if you do you will lose her forever."

Soon after, alas, the wife died. Lungelo was heartbroken, but he was always careful to obey his beloved wife's last words. Thanga, for that was what he named the child, grew up beautiful in body and spirit. Her father kept her indoors all day long, but at night, when the stars and moon rose high in the sky, Thanga went outside. There she worked so hard that Lungelo's crops flourished. His garden was the most beautiful in the village.

"Thanga, I am blessed," he said to his dear daughter. "You are a special child."

Soon people everywhere heard about Thanga. She was famous for her beauty, but more than that, people spoke of her diligence and hard work, and of the magic she made in the fields while all the others slept.

At night, beneath the shining silver moon, Thanga tilled and hoed and weeded. She sang as she worked, for she loved the songs of the tiny tree frogs. They were her chorus, and all night long as Thanga worked, she smiled to hear the sound of their throaty voices, singing until it seemed their throats would burst.

Before long a prince, the son of a faraway chief, heard about Thanga. He longed to meet her. "Surely a girl of such beauty and diligence combined would be a wonderful bride," he said to his father. And so he dressed himself in his finest clothes and set out to travel to Thanga's village.

He knew he had no hope of seeing her by daylight, so when he neared her home, he sat down at the spring to await the coming of night.

As the moon rose in the sky, he looked up and saw the girl come down the path. His heart swelled. She sang so beautifully, and her lovely face glowed in the moonlight. Her beads and bracelets set in silver caught the light of the stars and they glistened. Her teeth gleamed ivory white as she shyly smiled at this stranger who sat by the spring.

The prince could barely breathe at the sight of her. He felt suddenly shy and knew at once that he loved her. And Thanga, seeing him, felt her heart skip a beat. She knew she loved him, too.

The chief's son was determined to ask Thanga's father for permission to marry the girl. At dawn he went to see Lungelo. When Lungelo saw how radiant his daughter looked, he agreed to the marriage at once. And so the chief's son went happily home to announce his news to his father.

But the chief was not so pleased. "I have heard of this strange young woman," he said, " and I do not wish you to marry a girl who must sleep in the daylight. What will you do with a girl like that?"

When the chief refused, his son grew so unhappy that at last the chief's wife intervened. "Husband, our son will die of lovesickness if he does not marry Thanga." Finally, after some time, the chief agreed, and so, with great celebration, by the light of the moon, the prince and Thanga wed.

For several years life went on happily, and everyone loved Thanga. The chief, though, was suspicious. He did not believe that Thanga would vanish in the light of the sun, and secretly he determined to prove she was not telling the truth.

At last Thanga gave birth to a strong, healthy son. The prince and Thanga named the boy Dantalasele.

One sunny day, the prince went off to visit another village for a few days. Thanga and Dantalasele lay inside, behind closed shutters.

The chief called to Thanga. "Fetch some water from the spring, daughter-in-law. I need it now and no one else is here to do this chore."

Thanga looked questioningly at her father-in-law. "Father, it is daylight," she said. "Please, won't you wait until the sun has set? Then I shall happily fetch your water."

The old man grew furious. "I will beat you if you do not do as I bid," he said.

Thanga was an obedient girl, and her father-in-law would hear no argument. And so at last, Thanga sadly handed the child to him and said, "Care for Dantalasele while I am gone." Then she picked up the water jar and placed it upon her head. Off she walked, into the bright sunlight.

At the spring she dipped the gourd scoop into the water to fill the jar. Just as she did this, it slipped from her hand and sank, down, down, down.

Thanga shook her head and scolded herself, "Now why did the gourd slip from my hand?" For one moment she sat helplessly, and then she took off her head-covering. Holding this by four corners, she lowered it into the spring to draw up the water. But in an instant, the scarf slipped from her fingers, and down, down, down it went.

"What a clumsy girl I am!" Thanga cried. Again she looked helplessly about her and at last, even as the sun beat down on her, slipped out of her skirt. She made a bag of that and reached over and began to scoop water into the jar with it. But with a swirl and a swoosh, the bag slipped from her fingers. Down, down, down into the spring it went.

Now Thanga was partly naked, and still she had no water for her father-in-law. And how would she cover herself to go home? she wondered. Carefully she dipped the jar itself into the water, and water began to trickle into it. But just as it was nearly full, Thanga felt something tug it from her grasp. She struggled, trying to save it, but once her hand touched the water she felt something grab her fingers. It would not let her go.

Then—swoosh—Thanga too was pulled into the spring. Down, down, down she went, until she reached the spirits of the spring. They welcomed her and bade her stay, forever.

PART TWO

BACK IN the chief's house, Dantalasele grew hungry and began to wail. "Nurse," said the chief to the baby's nurse, "go to the spring and bring that lazy mother home to feed her child."

The nurse put the baby on her back and hurried to the spring. But not finding her mistress there, she returned to the chief. "I saw her footprints at the water's edge, but she is nowhere in sight."

Dantalasele grew hungrier still. Louder and louder he cried, and the chief could do nothing. When the chief's wife came home from the fields, she scolded her husband into the night. "How could you let her go? You know she must not see daylight." The mother-in-law tried to feed the baby warmed milk, but he spat it out and cried all the harder.

At midnight the nurse carried the child outside to try to comfort him. She walked toward the spring. Soon she began to sing, rocking the baby back and forth as she did:

Dantalasele is crying
The moon is shining;
The baby is crying!

When she reached the spring, she opened her eyes wide, for there she saw Thanga. The beautiful young woman rose out of the depths of the spring, stretching forth her arms. She took her child to her breast and Dantalasele drank until he was full and quiet once again. Then Thanga gave the boy back. "The spirits of the spring have claimed me, and they will never let me go."

In the morning the child was laughing and happy once again. The grandparents were puzzled. "What did you do?" they asked the nurse.

"Never mind," she said. "He has filled himself at the spring, and so he is no longer hungry."

And so each night, while everyone slept, the nurse walked with the child to the spring, singing as she walked:

> Dantalasele is crying
> The moon is shining;
> The baby is crying!

Each night Thanga rose from the depths and fed her child, played with him a while, and handed him back to the nurse, who hurried home.

After a few days the prince returned from his visit in a faraway village. When he heard what happened, he was distraught. The chief bowed his head in shame as he told his son what he had done.

"You have taken my wife from me!" the prince cried. Weeping, he held Dantalasele close to him and said, "At least I have our child."

When the nurse told him that the child was nourished by the waters of the spring, the prince did not believe her. One night he secretly followed her as she took her midnight walk.

The prince was amazed to see his beloved Thanga rise from the water at the sound of the song. He knew he must not show himself to her. He watched silently as Thanga fed their child.

81

With a heavy heart he returned home and told his mother what he had seen. "Wait until the moon is high and full," she said, "and then go and capture her."

When nightfall came, the prince went to the spring and hid himself in the long grass. Before long the nurse came down the path singing her song, and Thanga rose to the surface.

But this time Thanga seemed uneasy. She shivered as she took hold of her child. "Is someone there with you?" she asked the nurse.

At that her husband rushed forward and caught Thanga around the waist. He pulled with all his strength. Slowly, Thanga, her husband's arms around her, was released from the spring. But with her came the water. It roared and foamed and swirled around them, filling the path, flooding the fields. Higher and higher it rose until the chief's son feared that it would drown all the huts for miles around.

Then—swoosh—the force of the mighty water dragged husband and wife apart, leaving the child in his father's arms. And once again Thanga disappeared beneath the waters, which soon subsided.

The next night, when all was still once more, the husband went to the water's edge and called to his wife. Not one ripple broke the spring's surface.

At last, despairing, the young man called upon his ancestors for help. A huge copper bird flew out of the sky and landed beside him. "What is wrong, young prince?" the creature asked, and the chief's son told his tale.

"Through fear and respect for my father, Thanga disobeyed the orders of the underworld that her mother gave at her birth," said the prince. "Now, to punish her, the spirits have taken her to live with them at the bottom of the spring."

"Yes," said the bird, nodding; his copper head glinted in the moonlight. "I will help you, for you are being punished for your father's foolishness. Go now and fetch two fat oxen and a pitch-black bull. Such gifts will please the spirits of the spring."

The chief's son went directly home. Later, he drove the beasts to the edge of the spring and called to the copper bird. The bird swept down and met him and said, "Push the oxen into the spring." This the chief's son did. The strange bird climbed upon the back of the black bull and rode it into the spring.

For a long time there was silence. Then at last the water parted. There was Thanga, shining more beautifully than ever before! With joy her husband took her hand, and as the pink fingers of dawn flushed around them, the chief's son and Thanga went back home.

And one by one the spring tossed the gourd, the head-covering, the skirt, and the jar. When Thanga's mother-in-law went to the spring the next morning, she saw them lying there and knew that all was well.

Kerplunk

LONG AGO near a river in Australia, in a gum tree beside a shallow pool known as a billabong, a tiny possum was born. By summer she was eating sweet nectar from the many flowers. One day after eating, she climbed to the top of the gum tree to rest.

As she slept, a gum nut fell from the tree into the billabong below. Kerplunk!

Possum woke at once. Below her she saw the water shivering in the shade of the tree, and she began to shiver too. Without stopping to think, she climbed down the tree and ran as fast as she could, calling out loudly, "Run for your life! Kerplunk is coming to get us! Run for your life!"

Soon her mother and her father and all the other brush-tailed possums heard her cries. They too began to run. "Kerplunk is coming! Run! Run fast!" they cried as they chased Possum.

As they ran beneath a grove of eucalyptus trees, Koala heard their cries. Koala almost never hurried, but now she slipped down the tree, carrying her baby on her back. "Little possum, what's wrong?" Koala asked.

"Kerplunk is coming after us!" cried Possum. "Kerplunk is coming to get us. Run fast for your life!"

And Koala joined the race.

They ran and ran, calling out for all to hear, "Kerplunk is coming to get us!"

Soon they came to a wide, rocky cave. The dust they raised while

running flew into the cave, and out came Tasmanian Devil, grumbling, "What's all the commotion out there?"

Koala and Possum called, "Kerplunk is coming after us. Run for your life!" and Tasmanian Devil slowly lumbered out of his cave and ran along behind them.

Before long the group passed by a quiet stream where Platypus was taking a rest. "Run for your life!" Tasmanian Devil cried. "Kerplunk is coming after us." When Platypus heard the news, his long snout quivered and the spurs on his ankles stiffened. As fast as he could, he came out of the stream and ran along on his webbed feet.

"Kerplunk is coming after us!" cried Possum and Koala and Tasmanian Devil and Platypus. "Kerplunk is going to get us! Run for your life."

Now Goanna the lizard lifted her head from her afternoon rest when she heard the cries. "Kerplunk is coming after us," Platypus squeaked.

Goanna quickly crept beside the others, calling out, "Kerplunk is coming after us! Everyone run for your life!"

Before too long, Kookaburra swooped down from the skies. When he heard the cries, he began to laugh nervously and call to all the birds he saw, "Fly fast, for Kerplunk is coming after us."

Soon the air was filled with the flapping wings of many birds. Below them on the forest floor could be heard the sound of running feet—spiny anteaters and wombats and bandicoots. Even Emu was flapping his wings and crying, "Here comes Kerplunk! Look out!"

Now Wallaby heard the sounds. "Kerplunk is coming! Run for your life!" Wallaby thumped the ground with one of his hind legs and began to hop for his life, swinging his arms as he hopped. "Watch out, Kerplunk is coming!"

The forest floor rang out with thumping and pounding and flapping and crying and hopping, and Dingo raised his head into the air. "What's all this about Kerplunk?"

"Run away, run away," Possum cried as she led the chase. "Run fast!"

The thundering sound at last roused Kangaroo, who had been sleeping peacefully.

"What?" he asked, opening one eye, and then the other. He saw every creature he could imagine running toward him.

Kangaroo hopped out to the middle of the path to see what was happening.

"What's this?" he asked as the animals galloped by.

The fleeing herd of animals came to a halt.

"Run, Kangaroo, run!" Dingo howled. "Kerplunk is coming after us! We must run away!"

"Kerplunk is coming to get us," hissed Tiger Cat.

"The horrible Kerplunk is coming," mumbled Tasmanian Devil. "Koala gave me the news."

Kangaroo turned a wary eye on Koala.

"It was Possum who told me," whispered Koala. "Possum told me all about the danger."

Now Kangaroo turned and stared at little Possum. "Little Possum," he said very calmly, "what and who and where is this Kerplunk, whom you say is coming to get us?"

Possum was trembling and tried to catch her breath.

All the animals stood very still and waited, and the birds swooped close and hovered overhead to hear. Kookaburra laughed and laughed. "Tell us, Possum, tell us."

Once more, the forest was still and silent, and the only sound that could be heard was the soft summer wind blowing through the trees.

And just then, another gum nut dropped into another billabong.

Little Possum jumped two feet in the air. "There it is!" she cried. "There's Kerplunk! Kerplunk is coming after us."

Koala looked at Platypus, and he looked at Goanna, and she looked

at Wallaby, and he looked at Dingo, and every single animal looked at every other animal, and Kookaburra laughed and laughed.

Now they all understood just exactly what had happened. One by one they dropped their heads in shame, and they turned and looked at Kangaroo.

Kangaroo laughed quietly. "Little Possum," he said, "listen to me. The sound you heard is only the sound of our gum nuts falling into our waters. Be careful, little Possum. Next time you must see for yourself what is happening before you start such a stampede."

The animals began to laugh. But Kangaroo called for order.

"And you!" Kangaroo stared hard at the others. "Next time, each of you will think before you believe everything little Possum tells you."

All the animals agreed. "Yes, we will think," Wallaby said, and he thumped his leg hard.

"Yes, we will think," the others echoed.

And as for Little Possum, from that day on, she always made certain to sit and think a while before she jumped, and she lived a long and happy life.

Haoua and the Butterflies

LONG AGO, when the world had just begun, when all was amber and gold, there was a sweet-smelling garden, lush and beautiful and filled with glorious flowers of many colors and shapes. In this garden, which was known as Djenna, there lived a woman named Haoua.

Haoua was graceful and lovely, and every creature and plant loved her.

The roses especially loved Haoua, but one day they complained to Allah. "We want to have wings so that we can follow Haoua. We want to have wings like the bees so that we might brush against her cheeks and flutter about her honey-scented hair and walk with her always."

Allah heard their request but said nothing, and the roses did not grow wings.

Haoua did not pay much attention to the roses. She spent her days roaming through the garden. One day, she came upon a serpent in the grass. "Haoua," hissed the serpent, "Haoua . . ."

She looked down and saw the serpent encircling an almond tree. "Tell me, oh lovely one," said the serpent, whose name was Haia, "do you think you are less important than the angels?"

Haoua bent down and moved close to the serpent. "Oh no," Haoua said.

"Why then do you satisfy yourself with this simple garden?" Haia asked. "There is more to life than bubbling

fountains and the shade of palms. There is more to life than the sweet fragrance of flowers and the buzzing of bees."

Haoua sighed deeply. "I would like to know life and the whole wide world," she said, "but Allah has commanded me to stay forever in Djenna."

"Do not listen to Allah," said the serpent. "Do you not want to wander the world?"

Haoua listened carefully and considered the serpent's words. "Oh yes, Haia, I do," she answered.

For many days Haoua came to the almond tree and listened to Haia's tempting words and whispered secrets. "Out there, outside of Djena, there are many sights," Haia said. "Out there is a world you ought to see and smell and·taste. Out there is more than perfume, sun, and trees. Do you not wish to know what the angels know, Haoua?"

At last Haoua said, "I want to know the world. I will disobey Allah," and she closed her eyes and looked up at the sky. "I wish to leave Djenna," she said.

When Allah heard Haoua's wish, he condemned her to leave the perfect garden and to wander the earth forever.

When the roses heard that their beloved was about to leave the garden, they grew heavy and sad. Their petals wilted and hung low to the ground. Soon their tips grew brown and stiff. "We wish to share Haoua's exile," they cried to the angels. "We wish to follow her out into the world," they wept.

"But roses," said the angels, "why would you wish to leave the blessed garden?"

"Oh," the roses wailed, "without Haoua this garden will be too lonely. Without Haoua's presence we will have no joy. Without Haoua we shall die." Tiny droplets fell from their sweet centers and watered the earth.

The angels argued with the roses. "Out of the garden," they said,

"you will suffer. You will feel the cruel heat of the summer afternoon and you will know no shade. You will shiver in the biting cold of winter. You will tremble beneath the showers of spring."

"We would endure anything," said the roses, "but we cannot live without Haoua."

The angels gathered to discuss the matter. They spread their wings and huddled together, hovering over the roses. "They will not listen to us," whispered the angels. "They want to leave."

At last they decided what to do, and they flew down to the garden to tell the roses. "You shall follow Haoua forever," they said. "On the day Haoua leaves the garden, join us at the gates and we shall transform you."

The day for Haoua to leave the garden came soon. The roses, filled with joy, gathered behind her. The angels commanded them: Join your petals. And they did, two by two. In a moment they became butterflies.

"Follow Haoua," the angels called, and as Haoua stepped out of the Garden of Djenna, the bees and the birds and the other flowers cried out, "Do not leave us," but Haoua walked on, and the butterflies followed.

Now they flew behind her and caressed her cheeks. They gathered together and formed a crown around her head. "We are coming with you," they whispered to Haoua.

But Haoua did not notice them, for she was thinking of the serpent's words, so excited was she that at last she would discover all there was to see in the world.

The butterflies flew faster and called again to her. "Haoua, do you hear us? Hear us, we are coming with you," but Haoua waved her hand over her head, brushing the butterflies away.

They fluttered on, unhappily.

"We mean nothing to her," the butterflies said sadly. "She will not listen to us. Now we are alone in this unknown world, with no hope of returning to our paradise of Djenna."

And the butterflies were so sad that forever afterward they flitted from flower to flower.

The people, seeing the butterflies, say that they dance this way in search of someone to love. But the angels say that the butterflies are seeking the way back to the Garden of Djenna.

And only Allah knows the truth.

The Man Who Was a Mule

ONCE UPON A TIME in Spain, a young man named Jose sat with his friends. Jose and his friends were students, and they were very poor. This evening they sat together worrying about their sad state of affairs.

"We have studied so hard," said Juan, "and look what it has done for us. We have nothing!"

"Soon we will finish our schooling," said Pepe. "And then what will we do?"

For a long while the friends sat together, thinking of the many ways they might earn money. At last, after a long, long talk, Jose sat up quite suddenly and said, "I have a grand idea, friends! We will be rich!"

"And how is that?" laughed Pepe, for he knew that Jose was poorest of all of the boys. And he knew Jose was a trickster.

"I will be the Grandee of Spain!" said Jose.

His friends roared with laughter. "Hah!" cried Carlos, "What imagination you have, my friend!"

Jose grew quite serious and held up his hand. "You laugh, friends, but by this time tomorrow evening I shall return to you with a potful of coins!"

The very next morning at dawn Jose and Pepe set off down the road. "We are looking for a mule seller," Jose whispered. "Now do as I say." Pepe nodded.

Sure enough, soon the boys came upon a mule seller. He rode upon

a tall gray mule, and behind him came four more mules. These creatures were sad and slow and bruised black and blue.

"That man beats his creatures," whispered Pepe, and Jose nodded. The boys moved behind some tall bushes and bent down low.

A moment later, the mule seller passed by on the first mule, then came the second, the third and the fourth. Just as the fifth mule clip-clopped past, Jose jumped out onto the road and grabbed the mule and pulled it quickly behind the bush. He lifted off the saddle and the saddlecloth, the bridle and the lead. He turned to his friend. "Pepe," he said, "take this creature to the marketplace and sell him. Meet me back at school tonight and we shall celebrate!"

Pepe jumped upon the mule's bare back and quickly rode off. Then Jose placed the saddlecloth and the saddle upon his own back, and trotted onto the road and into line behind the other mules.

It was a very hot day and the road was dusty and long. The creatures walked, and they walked, and they walked. Soon the steady motion and the blazing sun rocked the mule seller to sleep. Jose ran ahead and stopped in front of the second mule. He held up his hand and the mules stopped. He ran back to the end.

At this the mule seller woke with a start. He listened hard. "I do not hear my mules," he said, and he turned and saw his mules stopped still. At once he trotted back to the mules. "Get going!" he cried. He whipped the first mule. "Move now!" he shouted to the second. "What is wrong with you stupid creatures!" he cried to the third, but when he reached to whip the fourth mule he stopped, for he saw that this mule was a man.

"What's this!" he cried. His face flushed and his heart began to pound. "What kind of trick is this?"

"I am your fifth mule," said Jose, very softly. "I have returned to earth in my own shape because my punishment has ended."

The mule seller opened his mouth very wide and he stared. "What can you mean?" he said. His voice grew softer, for he had never before met a mule in the shape of a man.

"Oh, let me explain," said Jose. "You see, my friend, many years ago I committed a crime and for this I was turned into a mule. But now, you see, I have paid for my crime, and my bewitchment has ended. I am back to being myself once again."

"But where is my mule?" cried the mule seller. "I paid a pretty price for that creature just three years ago."

"Oh," cried Jose, "you must understand, sir. I was that mule. That mule was me."

The mule seller squinted and stared. "Why didn't you tell me? Why didn't you speak to me before?'

"I was going to," said Jose. Then he paused and stared at the mule seller and he grew very serious indeed. "But you see, you were a cruel man. You beat me, and some days you did not feed me well. But never mind. I know that was my punishment. And now my punishment has ended."

The mule seller scratched his head and walked around Jose. "I do not understand," he mumbled, "I do not understand."

"It is simple," said Jose. "I am the mule you once bought, but I am now a man again and I have paid for my crime."

"Yes," mumbled the mule seller, circling Jose once more. "Yes, I always thought there was something very strange about that mule. I mean about you."

"Now," said Jose, "please take this saddle from my back. I've had enough! And from this day on you will know that once the Grandee of Spain was your slave, but now he is wealthy and powerful again!"

The mule seller gasped. "The Grandee of Spain!" he cried. At once he bent down on his knees. "Oh, good sir, good Grandee of Spain! Forgive me for all I did to you when you were a mule."

"You are forgiven," said Jose. "It is not your fault that you did not know who I was. And besides, I am a generous man."

"Oh bless you!" cried the mule seller. "Bless you!"

"But you must promise two things," said Jose as he helped the man to his feet. "First, you must promise to be kind to your creatures. Second, you must never tell a soul what has happened to me."

Weeks passed. Then the mule seller went to the marketplace to buy a mule to replace the Grandee of Spain who had once been his mule. "Good day, sir," said the mule seller to the auctioneer. "I've come to buy a mule."

"Friend," said the auctioneer, "what happened to the mule you owned?"

The mule seller stepped close to the auctioneer and whispered, "I had to sell him, friend. For personal reasons."

"Well," said the auctioneer, "if I were you I would buy him back. He's just over there," and he pointed to the far side of the marketplace.

The mule seller looked. Sure enough, he recognized his old mule's sad eyes and droopy ears. And he knew the strange look in his eyes. He quickly walked to the mule and he looked at him closely. "Yes, it is you," he whispered in the mule's ear.

The mule bent his head very low.

"I am so sorry, sir. You must have done a terrible deed to be turned back into a mule."

The mule looked up at him and the man recognized the mule's smile.

"Never mind," said the mule seller. "I will buy you once again. And this time I will treat you well, for I know you are the Grandee of Spain!"

The Pooka

ONCE UPON A TIME in Ireland, a farmer's son stood out in the still, bitter cold and looked after the family cattle. Suddenly he felt a gust of wind swoosh past him. Now the farmer's son knew what this was, for he knew that fairies dwelt nearby.

The boy was curious, for he had never seen a fairy. So he called out, "Hello, Pooka, won't you show yourself to me?" No answer came. "If you will, I'll give you my coat to keep you warm," he called. And whoosh, a big handsome bull appeared. The boy threw his coat over the bull, and in the next moment the creature turned gentle and quiet. And then the bull spoke. "Very well. Come to the mill tonight and I will give you some good luck."

That night the boy went to the mill. There, as always, he saw his father's workers, but all the men were fast asleep. "What's this," the boy asked, "has the Pooka fooled me?" There was nothing to do but to shrug and sigh and curl up to wait. And soon he fell asleep.

At dawn he woke and rubbed his eyes. He could not believe what he saw! The empty stacks brimmed with freshly ground corn. The boy looked around. All the men were still asleep. He scratched his head. "I know these men did not grind corn. It must have been the fairies," he said.

The next night he returned to the mill and once again he found the sleeping men. Again he curled up and fell asleep, and in the morning? Yes, again! Every single sack brimmed with fine meal.

"I must see the fairies work," said the boy, and then he spotted, in a corner of the mill, a big wooden chest. On the third night he returned and crept inside the chest and peeked through the keyhole to watch.

Ah! Just as the boy had expected. At midnight six small fellows crept softly into the mill. Each one carried a sack of corn upon his back, and behind them came one more, a tiny, wrinkled man dressed in tattered rags.

"Turn the mill now," said the man in tattered clothes, and all the little fellows began to turn. They turned and they turned, and soon every single stalk of corn was milled.

"So that is the Pooka," said the boy, pleased with himself.

He rushed to tell his father the tale. At first the farmer was suspicious, and so, that night, the lad took his father to the mill and together they climbed inside the dusty chest.

And sure enough, just after midnight the little fellows marched through the door and the old Pooka called out, "Grind the corn!" And grind they did.

"Ah," said the farmer, "so this is the good Pooka's work." The boy smiled. "Well, then," said the farmer, "let him work, for my men are idle. I shall send the lot of them off tomorrow and leave the grinding of corn for our fine friends."

And so he did. Soon the farmer spent no money on labor and still his farm prospered and grew. The farmer began to grow rich. The people in the village gossiped, but the farmer and his son kept their secret, for they knew that if they did not, they would lose their luck.

And so the years passed.

Many nights the farmer's son went to the mill and hid in the chest to watch the fairies work. Night after night they appeared, and ground, and ground, and ground. Night after night the old Pooka conducted his men. "On with it," he cried. "On with your work!"

But some nights were hard. Sometimes the little Pookas rebelled

and said, "No, we won't work!" Some nights the little pookas seemed out of sorts. Some nights the poor old Pooka lost his voice crying for the little ones to work.

The farmer's son, ever grateful to the old Pooka, took pity on him. "Our Pooka is so kind," said the lad to himself. "He is so good to us."

And so, one day, out of love and gratitude and pity, the farmer's son went to the village and bought a suit woven of beautiful fine silk. That night he took the suit to the mill and laid it upon the floor, just where the old Pooka would spot it. Then he crept into the chest.

When the old Pooka appeared and saw the suit of clothes, he cried, "What's this? Are these for me?" No one answered, of course. "So someone will make a fine gentleman of me," said the Pooka. Silence still. "What am I to make of that?" And then he took off his old, tattered clothes and put on the beautiful suit.

"Lovely," he cried. He pranced about the mill. "How very fine to be a gentleman," said he.

At dawn he remembered the corn. "Ah me!" he cried. "There's work to do." He turned to his little pookas and cried, "We must grind!"

But then! "Wait," said he. "Just one moment," and he touched the soft suit. "No more work for me!" The pookas stopped grinding and stared.

"Fine gentlemen do not grind corn. No indeed they do not," said the old Pooka. "I think I shall go out into the world and show off my clothes." And with that he rolled up his tattered rags and walked away. Off he went, into the world.

That night the farmer's corn was not ground, and the next night it was not, and the next. The farmer's son dearly missed the old Pooka. Off he went into the fields calling, "Pooka, my friend . . ." and this he did for many weeks. But never again in his whole life did the lad see that grand old Pooka, and never again did anyone hear a sound from the old mill.

Now, you might think that the farmer would be sad or angry, but he had made enough money. He sold the mill and raised his son to be a scholar. And he bought his son a fine house on the rolling green hills. Time passed.

The son remained a kind, generous lad, and soon he chose to wed a lovely, kind, generous woman.

Now at the wedding, just when all the people stood up to toast health, the groom looked across the room and saw a golden cup brimming with bubbling red wine. "Where did that cup come from?" he whispered to his father.

The farmer shrugged. He did not know.

"Where did the golden cup come from?" the groom asked his bride. But she had never before seen it.

The groom asked every single guest. Nobody knew. At last the farmer's son smiled and said, "It must have come from the Pooka," and he

drank from the cup and passed it to his bride to drink. And forever afterward the farmer's son and his bride lived happy lives.

To this very day the farmer's son's ancestors have kept that cup. And the Pooka's luck has stayed with them. They are prosperous and healthy and wise.

The Star Maiden

ONCE UPON A TIME there lived a young man beloved by his tribe and all the creatures of the earth. He was not only clever, he also had magic powers. He could turn himself into the shapes of different animals, trees, and flowers. He performed his magic so that he could better understand all living creatures. Often he wandered alone through the forest to observe their world.

One day he came upon a grassy meadow he had never seen before. Overhead he saw nothing but bright blue sky. At his feet wildflowers bloomed. The grass was as soft as feathers, and the whole place was haloed in light.

Filled with curiosity, he decided to wait to see who might come to tend the land. He turned himself into a tiny hare and lay in the grass, watching as the sun made its round in the sky.

After many hours, the sky grew soft and the stars above began to gleam. A full moon climbed in the sky and the croaking bullfrogs fell silent. The birds sang a lullaby. Soon all the forest creatures were fast asleep, and in the midst of the immense silence, he heard a beautiful song coming from the sky. Then suddenly a shadow fell over the meadow.

When the young man looked up, he saw a basket carrying seven maidens. Slowly the basket drifted to earth. The song grew louder, and soon he could clearly hear that the music came from the voices of the seven maidens. Their voices were as gentle as a breeze, as sweet as maple sugar, as

harmonious as the seasons. Louder still grew the song, and soon the basket landed with a soft swoosh.

The maidens stepped onto the earth and began to dance. Their smiles were as bright as the moonlight; their eyes glistened radiant as the sun. The young man stared in wonder. When his eyes fell upon the youngest maiden, he fell instantly in love. His heart beat hard as he watched the maidens dance among the flowers, still damp with evening dew. On and on they danced, singing so sweetly that soon all the creatures of the forest awoke to watch them.

All through the night they danced, but as the first morning star appeared in the sky, the maidens climbed into their basket. Up, up, up they floated, until they were invisible to all below.

All the next day the young man's mind was filled with visions of the star maiden. He again walked to the meadow. This time he turned himself into a tree. When at last the moon rose in the sky and the bullfrogs and birds quit their chatter, all was quiet for a few moments. Then he heard the sweet voices again.

Down, down, down floated the basket. Out climbed the seven star maidens. They danced and sang. Round and round they whirled, in and out, swaying, making music sweeter than the song of nightingales. Then suddenly the youngest maiden stopped beside the tree.

"Come here, sisters, and look," she said. "This tree was never here before." One by one the curious girls looked at the tree.

"This tree is magic," said the youngest maiden. "We must leave at once! Good magic or bad, we do not know, but this place is no longer ours alone."

The maidens jumped back into their basket and sailed up into the sky, following the moon's white path.

The young man was sad, for he wished to tell the star maiden he loved her. He wondered what to do as he watched the forest creatures play

in the morning sunshine. Then suddenly he spotted a field mouse and he smiled to himself. He sat down on the grass, whispered some magic words, and turned into a tiny field mouse. Then he sat still and waited throughout the day.

When the moon rose in the sky, the bullfrogs quieted, and all the other creatures fell silent. Once again the seven maidens in the basket drifted down to earth. Once again they climbed out and began to dance and sing. Hither and thither, round and round they danced. At last the little field mouse squeaked. "Look," cried the youngest maiden when she spotted the field mouse at her feet. "Come here and see this little creature," and she reached down to pet his glossy fur.

At that he squeaked a sad cry and the maiden's heart went out to him. "Do not be sad," she said as she tenderly lifted him and began to sing her beautiful song. With that the young man whispered two magic words and turned into a human again. He clasped the maiden in his arms.

"Sisters," she cried out, "help me! I am caught in this man's arms," but he held her fast. Carrying her, he quickly ran from the meadow into the forest. The youngest star maiden looked back and watched sadly as her sisters climbed into their basket. Up they rose, into the starry sky.

The young man hurried home with the star maiden in his arms. Soon afterward, she fell in love with him, for he was gentle and good to her. And they wed.

All the people of the tribe rejoiced, for they loved the young man and his star maiden. In the next season, the maiden gave birth to a boy, and for some time the family was happy.

Alas, after a while the maiden grew lonely, for though she loved her husband, when the stars glistened and gleamed she longed for her sisters up in the sky.

One day, while her husband was away hunting, the star maiden began to weave a basket. When she had finished, she carried her child to the meadow. There she climbed into the basket and began to sing. The basket floated up into the sky.

When the star maiden returned to her home in the sky, she was so happy that she soon forgot about the earth and her husband. She stayed in the sky and sang and danced with her sisters.

But as the young boy grew older, he began to feel out of place. His heart grew sad. When he looked at the face of the moon, he remembered his father. When he ran over the rainbows, he thought he could hear his father calling to him.

One day as he walked across the sky, he happened upon his mother's basket hanging from a star. He snatched the basket, climbed inside, and down he floated to earth. Sitting in the middle of the meadow was the boy's father. When he saw his son, his tears dried and he smiled, and father and son embraced. "Come with me," said the child. At once father and son climbed into the basket. Up they floated into the sky.

When the star maiden saw her husband, she remembered everything. "Dear husband," she said, "I am so happy in the sky, I forgot the earth. But I love you and wish we could be together still."

And so the star maiden and her husband decided that for one half of each year, they would live on earth, surrounded by the forest creatures, and for the other half they would live above, surrounded by the beings of the sky. In this way they were at peace on earth and in the sky.

The Fool and His Horse

ONCE UPON A TIME there lived a poor peasant who had three sons. The eldest two were handsome and proud, but the youngest was an idle lad who spent his days whiling away his time and resting by the fire. He was called Ivan the Fool.

The old peasant grew very sick one day. He called to his sons. "When I die," he said to them, "I wish you to take turns sleeping through the night at my grave. In this way I shall say my farewell." And then he died.

The first night after the funeral, the eldest son said to Ivan, "Take my place at our father's grave tonight," for the eldest son was frightened of the grave. Ivan went to the grave and lay down. At the stroke of midnight, the earth opened and the peasant rose from his grave. "Dear firstborn son, tell me, do the dogs bark and do the wolves howl, and do my children weep tonight?"

"Father, it is I, Ivan the Fool, and all is peace and quiet in Russia." At that his father sank into his grave and Ivan returned home.

On the second night the second brother turned to Ivan, and he said, "Go in my place, Ivan," for he too was afraid. So Ivan went to his father's grave, and at midnight the earth opened and the man rose from his grave and asked, "Is that you, my second son? Tell me, do the dogs bark and the wolves howl, and do my children weep tonight?"

"It is your son the fool," said Ivan. "All is peace and quiet in Russia tonight." The father returned to his grave, and Ivan walked back home.

On the third night Ivan took his turn and went to the grave. When midnight struck, the father rose out of his grave and asked, "Ivan, tell me, do the dogs bark and the wolves howl, and do my children weep tonight?"

"All is quiet in our land, father," said Ivan.

The father sighed deeply. Then he handed his son a bridle, and said, "Ivan, only you were brave enough to obey your father's wish. This is the bridle of a horse called Chestnut Gray. When the time comes, you must go out into the open fields and whistle once. Then call out, 'Chestnut Gray, hear and obey!' When the horse appears, you must climb into one of his ears and out the other. You will turn into the handsomest man in the world. Then mount the horse and ride wherever you will."

The father bid his son farewell and went to rest, forever, in his grave.

Years passed. The eldest sons grew prosperous, but Ivan only sat by the fire, whiling the time away.

Then one day the king announced that he was seeking a husband for his daughter, the fair Princess Katarina. He built her a tower twelve oak logs high. At the top of the tower, his daughter sat in a window, awaiting the man who could fulfill her father's wish.

"He who can leap upon his steed as high as my daughter's tower and plant a kiss upon her lips shall wed the fair princess," announced the king.

From far and wide the men of the land came to try their luck. Ivan's brothers took the finest, strongest steeds and off they galloped, leaving Ivan in their dust.

Ivan took his father's bridle and went out into the fields. He whistled once. Then he cried out, "Chestnut Gray, hear and obey!"

A bold, enormous steed came galloping across the field. When Chestnut Gray reached Ivan, he halted at once and Ivan reached up and stroked the horse's mane. Then he climbed into one enormous ear and slipped out the other, and when he emerged he was as handsome a knight as was ever seen. Ivan mounted the horse and off they set across the fields, quick as the wind. At last they reached the palace.

The grounds teemed with people. In the center of the field stood a tower twelve tall oak logs high. Ivan looked up, and up, and up, and he saw the beautiful Katarina. Ivan watched as one after another, the many suitors climbed upon their horse's back and leaped into the air. But alas, not one reached the princess.

Then came Ivan's turn. With a whoop and a shout, he prodded his horse, and Chestnut Gray spewed fire from his nostrils. Smoke poured from his enormous ears. He leaped to the window. Ivan planted a kiss on Katarina's lips. She reached out and struck his forehead with her ruby ring, leaving her seal there.

Ivan and Chestnut Gray landed upon the ground and rode away in a great cloud of dust. "Stop them!" called the king, and all the people gave chase, but alas, Chestnut Gray and Ivan were gone.

Off they rode into the open plains. Then Ivan climbed off his horse's back and through the great gray steed's ear and out the other. Once again, he was Ivan the Fool. The horse ran free.

Ivan returned home and tied a rag around his forehead to hide the ruby seal's mark. When his brothers returned, they told him of the strange and handsome knight who had stolen a kiss from the princess. "Oh, he was fine, and his fiery steed was most amazing!"

"Perhaps that was me," Ivan said.

His brothers roared. "You are a fool, brother," they said. "Sit by your fire and dream as you will." Ivan smiled to himself and went to sleep.

Soon the king held a great feast. He invited all his subjects to attend. "Take me with you, brothers," Ivan said, as they mounted their steeds to attend the king's feast. Again they laughed. "You are far too ugly and fool-ish," they said. "Go and sit by your fire and be idle." Then they were gone.

But Ivan was a determined fellow, and so, off he set on foot to the palace. At last he arrived. He sneaked into the banquet hall and sat in a corner while Katarina moved through the room, searching for the mark of her seal.

She finally came to Ivan. When she saw him she frowned, for he was filthy and tattered, and his hair stood on end. Oh, what a fool, she thought, but Katarina was a kindhearted girl. Seeing the fool's brow bound with a rag, she leaned close and asked, "What has happened to your head?"

"I fell and cut myself," Ivan said.

"But the rag is dirty," said Katarina, and she reached out and untied it.

At once a bright glow caught her eye. "That is my ruby seal," she cried. "Look, people, the noble knight sits here!"

The people turned and stared. The king quickly walked to the corner and stared. "No, my daughter, this cannot be your husband. He looks to me to be a fool!"

"Please give me a moment," said Ivan, "and I will wash my face. Then you shall see I am a good man after all."

With that he ran out to the courtyard and whistled once and called to Chestnut Gray. The noble steed came galloping like the wind toward him.

"Good Chestnut Gray," said Ivan, petting his mane, and then he climbed into one ear and out the other, and once again he was the handsomest knight in all the land.

Ivan ran back to the banquet hall. There the guests all turned and gasped, for this was no fool at all. This was the man who had kissed the princess.

"You shall wed," said the king, and Katarina kissed her beloved. And the two eldest brothers knew, then, what it meant to sleep beside their father's grave.

The Long-Nosed Boy

ONCE UPON A TIME there lived a poor lad who had no family and no fortune. One lovely summer day, he wandered through the forest as he always did, and that night he lay down to sleep beneath the trees. In the morning he reached up and picked a fig that grew on a tree nearby. He sighed deeply as he bit into it, for it was sweet and ripe. Then he leaned over to put on his shoes.

To his amazement, he bumped his nose upon his shin.

"Ouch," he said, rubbing his nose. "Why did that happen?" He opened his eyes wide and touched his nose. At once he realized something was wrong. "My nose," he cried. "My nose!"

His nose was three feet long.

What on earth am I to do now that my nose is three feet long, he thought. He wanted very much to be a well-liked man, and with his long nose he worried that people would never like him. He wondered what to do. As he sat thinking, he grew hungry again, and so he picked another fig and began to eat it.

When he finished eating the fig, he felt his nose begin to itch. He reached out to rub it, but now his nose was short again, right up close to his face, the way it had been before this whole story began.

"Ah," he said to himself. "Now I know exactly how to make my fortune," and he began to pick the figs as fast as he could. He filled his trouser pockets, his socks and shoes, and his broad straw hat, and then, as fast as you can say "three-foot nose," he dashed to the nearest town to sell his fruit.

"Figs for sale!" he cried, hurrying through the market square. "Figs for sale!" And before the sun reached the top of the sky, the lad had sold all of his figs.

Then he ran to the forest again. He found some goats grazing nearby, and smiled to himself. He clipped some of their hair, and with this he made himself a long, gray beard. He turned his clothing inside out. Then he gathered some more figs and built a fire. All night long he stirred his figs until he had made a thick, slimy fig paste.

In the morning he hobbled slowly into the village. "What's this?" he said as he walked through the crowds of people. "All these people here have noses that are three feet long! What's going on?"

A fellow who was selling baskets in the market said sadly, "Some rascal came to town yesterday and sold us fresh figs. Now everyone who ate one of his figs has a nose that's three feet long."

"Well, well," said the lad, stroking his beard and speaking in a voice so deep he sounded very old, "your people are lucky, good sir, for I have the remedy for this very trouble."

"You mean you can make noses short?" the man asked him, and at once he ran to tell the innkeeper the news.

A moment later the innkeeper, with a big belly and a nose even bigger, and his pretty young daughter with her long nose, and even their little dog, whose nose was as long as his body, stood before the lad dressed as an old man. Behind them came the barber and the baker and a painter and a poet. "Can you cure our noses?" they all clamored.

The lad stroked his long, gray beard. "It will cost you," he said.

"We'll pay anything!" they all said as they pulled more and more coins out of their pockets.

The lad took a bottle from his sleeve. In this he had placed the fig paste. He rubbed some paste on the end of the innkeeper's nose, and on his daughter's nose, and on the dog's, and in a moment their noses were as short as they had been before.

"Oh, you are our hero!" cried the innkeeper's daughter. Soon the word spread, and every man and woman and child with a long nose came to buy the magical paste.

They lined up, up and down the narrow street, and they filled up all the space in the whole village, for, you see, the people needed lots of room because they had such long noses. All day long they handed the lad their money, and all day long he rubbed paste onto their noses. By evening there was just one long nose left in the village, and that was the nose of the innkeeper's wife.

"To cure her nose," said the old man, "I ask in return but one thing. I wish to marry your daughter."

"Never!" cried the innkeeper, and so the lad turned around and walked away, and disappeared into the forest.

The next day the lad, dressed in a long robe he had woven of sheep's wool, wound a cloth around his head. This time he covered his face with more goat's hair, and he walked to the innkeeper's place. "What a long nose your wife has," he said, using an accent that made him a little difficult to understand.

"Oh, I am a stubborn man, and foolish too. A man of science offered to cure my poor wife if only he could marry my daughter. Woe is me! I refused, and now my wife cannot even turn around in her own home. Life is very unpleasant, as you can imagine."

"I can cure her nose," said the lad in his disguise.

"You can?" the innkeeper asked eagerly.

"Yes, easily," said the lad, "if you will just leave me alone with her for a little while."

"What do you want in exchange?" asked the innkeeper.

"I would like to marry your daughter," said the lad.

"Agreed," said the innkeeper. "That is, if she will have you. Once I was a fool, but now I am no longer," and he showed his wife into the room.

Alas, this time the wife refused to allow the man to marry her daughter. "Never!" she said. "Never someone from another land!"

And so the lad turned around and began to leave the house.

But just then the innkeeper's daughter ran into the room. "I don't care if he's a stranger," she cried. "I don't care who he is. If he is good enough and kind enough and wise enough to cure my mother, I can think of no one better to be my husband."

The lad smiled, and he rubbed a little paste on the end of the wife's nose, and poof, her nose was as short as it had ever been.

Then the lad took off his disguise, and he and the innkeeper's daughter smiled at each other, and they both knew that they would love each other well. Not long after, they were wed and lived happily ever after.

The Giant and the Paradise Islands

ONCE UPON A TIME in ancient China, the spring rains fell heavily. The raging rivers were filling; the water rose in all the streams. And all the rivers flowed to the great sea in the east.

The High God Tiandi, Emperor of the Heavens, looked down and smiled upon the land, for he knew that his people were safe. To the far east of the land, east of the eastern sea, there lay a great, wide gulf. The gulf was endlessly deep, forever wide, so huge that it could hold all of the world's waters. There the raging rivers and streams flowed. Tiandi knew that no matter how hard the rains fell, the sea would never overflow.

Upon the calm, blue gulf there floated five islands. These were the Paradise Islands, and on their shores grew magical trees that bloomed with glistening pearls. Birds of brilliant white fluttered about on the islands. And there immortals and lower gods lived in peace and happiness. They built palaces of smooth, cool jade and sparkling towers of gold, and they ate the fruit that grew in abundance.

There was but one problem on the islands. They floated. They wandered. Sometimes, tossing hither and yon, they bumped against each other, and sometimes they moved so far out to sea that the islanders worried that they might become forever lost. During the stormy seasons, the islands tumbled this way and that, tossing the islanders from one end of their island to another.

At last the islanders grew weary of the islands' wandering ways, and so they went to ask Tiandi for his help. "For our safety and our peace of mind," they said to the High God, "we ask that you root our five islands."

Tiandi listened, and he thought. The gulf had no bottom, no earth or sand or rock beneath its deep, fresh waters. "There is no bottom," said Tiandi. "There is nothing to which I can root your islands."

When the gods and immortals looked displeased, Tiandi said, "Let me think." And he thought some more. At last, after many moons, he knew what he must do. "You will be happy now," he told the immortals, "for I have sent five giant turtles to you. I have placed your islands upon the backs of the turtles, and now they will not rock and tumble in the stormy seas."

Back and forth swam the giant turtles. They moved slowly, steadily, carrying the Paradise Islands. And once again the islanders felt peaceful and happy.

Alas, one day a giant happened upon the wide gulf, and having no idea where he was or what this place could be, he smiled to himself. "So much water," he said. "I think I shall fish."

With one great stride the giant stepped across the gulf to one island. Then he sat upon a giant rock and cast his giant fishing rod out to sea.

Out, out, out went the line, across the waves, over the glistening foam, all the way over the curve where the sea met the sky. He sat and sat, idly moving the rod this way and that. He yawned and the sky above thundered. He shifted and the island trembled.

At last the giant, half-asleep, woke with a start, for he felt a tug upon his line. "A fish!" he cried. He began to pull.

The giant was strong, but even he struggled with all his might to pull in his long fishing line. "It's so heavy," he said in his thundering voice. "I

have found the catch of the world!" He pulled harder. Then, as his line moved toward him he slowly made out in the distance a strange sight indeed. He smiled to himself, for he could see that his line pulled in something enormous, something fabulous. He tugged harder.

At last the catch came into sight: two great turtles, upside down, their giant legs flailing in the air. They struggled to pull from the line, but it was no use. The giant had caught them and the line had flipped them upside down.

Now the islands were beneath the waters and the islanders gurgled and groaned. "Our world has turned upside down!" they cried as they watched the waves cascade over their jade pillars and golden domes. They wept to see their trees weeping the lovely white pearls. The pearls floated out to sea and disappeared, as did the great white birds.

Meanwhile, on the third island, the giant pulled so hard the turtles at last slipped to shore. Grinning with glee, the giant snatched them from the lines and, sticking one in each pocket, he stood and took one stride back to earth. Then he went off to cook his mighty turtle stew.

The islanders beneath the sea quickly went to the heavens to see the High God Tiandi. "How could you do this to us? You have let the giant destroy our turtles, and now we have lost all our peace. Our pearls have disappeared. Our castles are filled with water. Do something, Tiandi. You have destroyed our blessed islands. Do something!"

Tiandi, though the Highest God, could not destroy the giant. Still, he felt sorry for the islanders, and so again he sat and thought. "I cannot save your turtles," he said, "for they are gone."

The islanders wept and fretted.

Tiandi thought a while longer, and at last he smiled and said, "I cannot destroy the giant, but I shall make him smaller, and the three remaining islands will be safe and stable resting upon the backs of their giant turtles."

At this the immortals nodded, happy to know that others would not suffer as they had.

And so, to this day, the three remaining islands float upon the backs of the great turtles. They are called Penglai, Fanghu, and Yingzhu, and it is there that immortals and blessed men and women go to find peace from the worries and woes of the world.

Cats in the Well

ONCE UPON A TIME a wicked witch lived at the bottom of a deep, dry well. She spent her days inside that well with her ninety-six cats. She had collected them to help her with her witchcraft, and for a while they earned their keep. She sent them off to perform evil deeds, and when they returned home, she fed them treats. When the moon shone full and bright, the cats sat up—all ninety-six—and they howled like the north wind.

Years passed, and all went well, but by and by, the cats grew spoiled and lazy. One night the huge orange tom with shining yellow eyes set up a howl. He scratched at the witch's legs.

"What is it you want?" the witch cried angrily.

"Bring me some sweet whipped cream," he howled. "I want my cream, and now!"

"And me crabmeat!" squealed a tabby. "I want me crabmeat!"

"That's difficult," the witch began, for it is hard indeed to come by special treats when you live down a well.

An old Manx scratched at the witch's bare toes. "I want a shepherd's pie!"

"And tender steak," wailed a Siamese.

"And shrimps and chicken breasts," another howled.

Soon all ninety-six cats were wailing. "Give me lobster and deviled eggs." "We must have mustard and mayonnaise and melons." "And Stilton cheese and rabbits' feet." "And scallops and sole and sherbet."

The witch put her hands to her ears. She kicked and flailed her arms. "Stop it," she cried. "Stop your demands! I'll give you your treats if only you will stop your howls."

But they did not.

Soon the witch was at her wits' end. She climbed like a beetle up the rope, and when she reached the top of the well, she sat down to think. She longed to be rid of those cats.

Soon a pleasant young man happened by. He was riding on a lame horse and his clothes were shabby, but when he saw the poor witch wailing and moaning, he came to a quick halt, for he had a generous heart.

"What seems to be amiss, good mother?" he asked.

"Ninety-six cats!" said the witch gloomily.

The young man laughed. "That's quite a few."

"Oh, how I long to have fewer," said she.

"Perhaps next time you look, there'll be fewer."

The witch's yellow eyes lighted up. "If you can rid me of my cats," she said, "I'll give you a new horse and a purse full of gold."

The young man raised his eyebrows in surprise. "You don't look like a wealthy woman."

"Never mind that," cackled the witch. "Get rid of my cats and I'll reward you well."

The young man shrugged and said, "I'll do me best." After he had asked a few questions, he looked down at the witch and said, "Go down into your well and tell your brood they're all invited to a great feast at the inn over the hill."

The witch agreed and slid down the rope. When she told the cats of the fine invitation, they set up a howl of complaint.

"We're tired. We don't want to climb up the rope." For you see, the cats had grown very lazy.

The witch sighed and trembled with anger, but she was determined.

"Very well, I'll carry you," she said. All night she climbed the rope, carrying cats up, two by two. At last she had them all up at the top, and they set off toward the inn.

When the cats smelled the delicious aroma wafting from the inn, their whiskers stood on end. "Ahh, I smell lobster bisque and lemon pie." "And I smell salty cod and stew." They trotted still faster.

The young man stood outside the door to welcome the brood to the feast. They looked inside and saw, spread out on a long table, a feast such as none had ever before seen. They meowed and purred and licked their lips.

"Help yourselves, ladies and gentlemen," said the young man. "There's plenty here for all." With that he beckoned them inside.

Now the cats were so greedy that they did not notice a great pan filled with holy water that stood just inside the door. They rushed for the table, and as they did, each cat, one by one, fell into the pan. It was a horrid sight, for as soon as one touched the holy water, a hiss and a puff of smoke rose up and a fiery-eyed demon shot right up through the chimney!

You see, the man had guessed the truth. These were not real cats. They were but wicked spirits in disguise. The holy water changed them into their true form, and after that, they were never again seen in those parts.

"I'm most grateful," said the witch to the young man, and she handed him a purse heavy with gold. "Now I'll go to see about a horse," she said, "for I always keep my word."

"Come in for a bite to eat first," said the generous young man.

"Thanks," said the witch, trembling, "but I think not. You see, I'm not overfond of that stuff," and she pointed at the pan of holy water.

That moment they heard a squeal. "Help me!"

The witch and the young man whirled around and looked into the pan. There they saw a tiny black kitten, swimming madly about in the pan.

"Help, please," squealed the poor, drowning creature.

The young man quickly pulled the cat from the water. She sat and began to lick herself dry.

"What on earth?" asked the witch. "How did you come to be there?"

The little cat looked up and said, "If you please, Mother, I'm not a demon. I'm a real cat. The holy water didn't hurt me, though I'll tell you, I don't much like water."

The witch squinted and thought hard as she looked at the tiny black cat. "Hmm," she said at last, "how would you like to be a horse?"

"Not much," said the cat "unless I must."

The young man bent down and picked up the poor cat. "Let her be," said he. "She is just fine as a cat."

"Very well," said the witch, "I'll just run off and find you one of the enchanted horses from the Stable of the Storm." And off she went.

People say the witch and the black cat lived happily together ever afterward at the bottom of the well. And they say when you listen closely on a wild night, you can hear the sound of spirited galloping.

The Merchant's Camel

ONCE UPON A TIME a great king ruled over a large, prosperous land. The king was known far and wide for his wisdom and his generosity, and all the people of his land loved and admired him. During this good king's reign, the cow and the jaguar drank side by side at cool, shady pools, and the butterfly and snake lay eggs in the same nest. When the land was dry, rain fell, and when the fields were thick with mud, the sun burst through the clouds and dried the earth. Flowers and plants and people blossomed and bloomed.

Now one day a merchant lost his prize possession. He lost his favorite camel. He searched high and low for his beast. He searched day after day. Alas, after many, many weeks, having no luck, he ventured out across the borders of the land. "Perhaps she has wandered far away," he said to himself, and off he went.

After many days he came upon four men walking in the opposite direction. "Ho there," said the merchant, as he crossed the men's path. "Where do you travel?"

"We are unhappy men," said the first man. "We are ministers in our own land, but our land is ruled by a cruel and unjust king. We have decided to seek another place to live."

"I see," said the merchant.

"And you?" they asked. "Why is it you are wandering?" the first minister asked.

"I have lost my poor camel," said the merchant. "I am off to see if I can find her somewhere in this great, wide world. Let me ask you this, kind sirs. Have any of you seen a camel in your journeying? I doubt it, of course, and soon I think I will give up my search."

The ministers gathered together. They bowed their heads and spoke together, in whispers. The merchant stood nearby.

He leaned forward to try to hear what the men said. "Have you seen her?" he asked again. "Tell me what you whisper about. Tell me please what it is that you know."

"My name is Bodhadita," said the first minister. "And I wish to ask you something, kind sir."

"Anything." said the merchant. His heart began to beat wildly, for the four men seemed to be wise and good and fair.

"Was your animal, your camel, lame, good sir?" asked Bodhadita.

"Yes, she was!" cried the merchant. Now he was truly excited. "Yes, yes, yes! Oh, where have you seen my camel?"

But Bodhadita simply closed his eyes and fell silent, and the second minister stepped forward to speak. "And was your camel blind in one eye?" asked Bodhachandra, for that was the second man's name.

"Oh, yes!" cried the merchant. "She was blind and lame, but such a lovely creature. Oh won't you tell me where you have seen my camel, good sir?" But at that Bodhachandra fell silent and closed his eyes. The third minister stepped forward. He touched his hand to the merchant's shoulder andsaid, very softly, "Tell me, sir, was your creature's tail unusually short?"

"Stop teasing me!" shouted the merchant. "Tell me where you saw my camel! Tell me where she has gone now!"

But now it was Bodhavyapka's turn to close his eyes, and the fourth minister, whose name was Bodhavibishana, stepped forward. He

bowed low and spoke as softly as his friends. "I believe your camel may have had a cough, good sir? Could that be so?"

"I have been teased enough," the merchant wept. "You men are cruel, for you know everything about my poor lost camel. Tell me now where my creature has gone?"

"I am so sorry," said the first minister, "but none of us has seen your camel anywhere."

"You play with me!" cried the merchant.

The second minister smiled gently. "We do not tease or play," he said. "None of us has seen your camel. We have only observed her."

"What can you mean?" cried the merchant as he pulled at his hair and stamped his feet. "Tell me what you mean!"

"Follow us," said the four ministers. "We are on our way to your land to see your king. Let him explain to you what we have discovered on our journey."

"I am certain you have stolen my animal," hissed the merchant, "and now you ask me to go home, defeated and without my finest possession."

The ministers smiled again.

"Come with us," they urged the merchant, and at last, lost and sad, he fell silent and followed the four ministers to the land where butterfly and snake, cow and jaguar lived in peace.

The five men approached the castle. "Here I will find justice," said the merchant as he moved quickly up the marble steps. "Our ruler is a kind and just man!"

"That is what we hope," said the ministers, and all five men appeared before the king.

"Tell me what it is you need," said the king.

And quickly the merchant told the king of the men's findings. "I believe they have stolen my camel," he said.

The king sat up straight, "You have described this creature perfectly," he said. "Tell us how it is you know all about the camel."

The first minister bowed to the king. "Good sir, when I first saw the creature's tracks, I noticed that one of the footmarks was deeper than the others. That is how I knew he must be lame."

"And I," said the second minister, "observed that the leaves on one side of the road were snapped, while the others grew abundant and green. I knew then that the animal was blind in his right eye, for clearly he did not see the fruits of the trees on the right."

"I see," said the king. "And you?" he asked, and he turned to the third minister. "How did you know that the creature's tail was short?"

"Upon the road I saw small drops of blood," said the third minister. "And I realized that the flies and mosquitoes and gnats had bitten her but her tail was too short to shoo them away."

"Ahh," said the king. And he smiled. "And you, sir, how could you know of the camel's illness?"

"I observed that the hind leg prints scarcely touched ground. And so I knew that the camel must have contracted in pain."

"Ah," said the king, and then he turned to the merchant and said, "I will pay for the loss of your camel as she seems to be lost for good. And you," said the king, turning to the ministers, "please stay and be my counselors for you are observant, keen, and wise."

And so the four ministers came to help the great king of India. The merchant gathered all the people, and together they said a prayer for the lost camel, and together they praised their good king and the wise ministers.

There is an ancient saying in Islam: "Faith is the lost camel of the Believer." Some people say that this phrase originates from this tale, the lost camel representing man's faith, its traces visible only to those who observe carefully, and to those who use their powers wisely.

Good Night

AND NOW Moon began to grow tired and pale
  And he feared that his eyesight would very soon fail.
"Bear, I'm afraid, friend, I'm through for tonight."
"Oh no!" cried sweet Bear, "please don't turn out the light."

But Moon smiled sleepily down at his friend
Who had finished his plea. "Now the tale's at an end
For tonight, my dear Bear, for tonight that is all.
I will take you home now, but next month I will call.

"For Bear, you must wait, you must think of the others.
They wish to hear stories—all your sisters and brothers.
All your cousins and everyone out there tonight
Will wish me to read them a story 'neath my light.

"And so," Moon told Bear, "once each month I will come
To your room, to your window, just after the sun
Has set for the day and the stars are so bright.
Then you and I, Bear, will again take a flight.

"And I'll tell you the story of the little mouse queen,
And I'll tell you the story of a fairy's fine dream,
And I'll tell you the story of the Cats in the Well,
And I'll tell you the story of the Merchant's Camel."

"Oh, yes," said tired Bear, whose eyes were now closing.
For you see, our friend Bear had taken to dozing.
As they sailed back to Bear's room and Bear's little bed
Where Moon set Bear down, a soft pillow 'neath his head.

And came the next morning, Bear smiled at the sky,
And he knew up there somewhere, Moon was waiting to fly
To everyone's house and to everyone's room
To bring everyone stories, to lift away gloom.

And now Bear sat down with his bear and said
"I think I'll try reading to you, bear, instead
Of waiting for Moon. Now this is a try,
I'm going to read you this sweet lullaby:"

Tell me a story under the stars.
Tell me a story from near and afar
Tell me a story from every land.
Tell me a story—oh stories are grand!